Jennifer Johnst... born in Dublin in 193... novels include *The Old Jest*, w... ... int... *Captains and the Kings*, winner of the *Evening Standard* Best First Novel Award and the *Yorkshire Post* Award for the Best Book of the Year, and *Shadows on Our Skin*, which was shortlisted for the Booker Prize. She won a Lifetime Achievement Award at the Irish Book Awards in 2012.

David Foldvari is an illustrator living, working and teaching in London. He was born in Budapest in '73, and moved to the UK in the eighties. He studied at Brighton and then later at the Royal College of Art. He has been working as an illustrator since the late nineties, and in that time has worked for countless clients and publications. David specializes in editorial work, and his images are published weekly in the *Observer* alongside columns by Stewart Lee and David Mitchell. www.davidfoldvari.co.uk

JENNIFER JOHNSTON

How Many Miles to Babylon?

PENGUIN BOOKS

For David

PENGUIN ESSENTIALS

UK | USA | Canada | Ireland | Australia
India | New Zealand | South Africa

Penguin Books is part of the Penguin Random House group of companies
whose addresses can be found at global.penguinrandomhouse.com.

First published in Great Britain by Hamish Hamilton 1974
Published in Penguin Books 1988
This Penguin Essentials edition published 2016
001

Printed in Great Britain by Clays Ltd, St Ives plc

A CIP catalogue record for this book is available from the British Library

ISBN: 978-0-241-97897-9

www.greenpenguin.co.uk

MIX
Paper from
responsible sources
FSC® C018179

Penguin Random House is committed to a
sustainable future for our business, our readers
and our planet. This book is made from Forest
Stewardship Council® certified paper.

BECAUSE I am an officer and a gentleman they have given me my notebooks, pen, ink and paper. So I write and wait. I am committed to no cause, I love no living person. The fact that I have no future except what you can count in hours doesn't seem to disturb me unduly. After all, the future whether here or there is equally unknown. So for the waiting days I have only the past to play about with. I can juggle with a series of possibly inaccurate memories, my own interpretation, for what it is worth, of events. There is no place for speculation or hope, or even dreams. Strangely enough I think I like it like that.

I have not communicated with either my father or mother. Time enough for others to do that when it is all over. The fait accompli. On His Majesty's Service. Why prolong the pain that they will inevitably feel? It may kill him, but then, like me, he may be better off dead. My heart doesn't bleed for her.

They are treating me with the respect apparently due to my class, and with a reserve due, I am sure, to the fear that I may be mad. How alarmed men are by the lurking demons of the mind!

Major Glendinning has not been near me, a blessing for which I am duly grateful. He will never make a man of me now, but I don't suppose he'll lose much sleep over that. There were moments when I almost admired him.

By now the attack must be on. A hundred yards of mournful earth, a hill topped with a circle of trees, that at home would have belonged exclusively to the fairies, a farm, some roofless cottages, quiet unimportant places, now the centre of the world for tens of thousands of men. The end of the world for many, the heroes and the cowards, the masters and the slaves. It will no doubt be raining on them, a thick and evil February rain.

The padre comes to visit me from time to time. He showed me yesterday the gold cross he wears under his viyella vest, pressing into the black hairs that seem to ramp over his chest.

'Have you Faith?' he asked me.

He didn't put it quite like that. He had a more sophisticated way of phrasing things, and also a certain embarrassment in asking what he made sound like an almost indecent question.

'I've never really thought about it.'

'Now is perhaps the time to think.'

I wished that he would go away. I was not, nor am I now, in the mood for soul wrestling, that is a pastime for those who have time to spare.

'It's a bit late now I fear, Padre. Faith is to comfort the living. It seems to me to be irrelevant for the dead.'

'You are alive.'

'Technically.'

'Comfort perhaps . . .'

'I am comfortable, thank you. I . . . I wonder always why you . . . you know . . . you . . .' I put out my hand and touched his dog collar, 'well, representatives, seem to get such satisfaction in making us afraid of death. Be joyful in the Lord. Come before his presence with a song. That's not quite right, I know, but the drift is there. I shall sing gladly.

How many miles to Babylon?

Four score and ten, sir.

Will I get there by candlelight?

Yes and back again, sir . . .'

I croak rather than sing. He held a hand up in distress.

'Your frivolity makes me uneasy.'

'I'm sorry. No need. We all must have our own way of dying.'

He pushed the cross back in through his shirt and fastened

2

it up. He left soon after. I was sorry that I had distressed him.

As a child I was alone. I am making no excuses for myself, merely stating a fact. I was isolated from the surrounding children of my own age by the traditional barriers of class and education. Not that I was educated in any formal way. A series of ladies taught me a series of subjects until at the magic age of ten I was handed over to the curate who, presumably to supplement his tiny income, spent several hours each day trying to teach me mathematics, English literature, a smattering of French grammar, and of course Latin. Latin was his subject and his face would begin to glow with pleasure as the moment arrived for us to open up one of the numerous books we translated together. On days when I felt particularly unkind I would fumble and stumble over the words and watch maliciously the visible disintegration of his pleasure. He smelt delicately of peppermints. Once every hour or so two of his white fingers would probe into his waistcoat pocket and pull out the small white sweet which he would slip into his mouth almost as if he were performing some minor criminal act.

There was also the piano teacher who used to come down once a week on the train from Dublin. I remember little about him except for his ineffectiveness as a teacher and the reason for his going. My mother would come into the drawing-room towards the end of each lesson and sigh restlessly from her chair, fretted by my lack of progress. He was a nervous man who became almost insane in her presence. His hands would shake, and he would begin to tear distractedly at the dark stains of hardened food that decorated the front of his jacket as he watched me play. The drawing-room smelt of apple-wood and turf, and, in the autumn, the bitter end-of-the-year smell of chrysanthemums which stood in pots massed in one of the deep bay windows, shades of yellow, gold, bronze and white, like a second fire in the room. The black ebony case of the Steinway grand reflected the flowers. The music teacher

3

was ridiculously out of place.

He rose and approached my mother, bowing at her as he crossed the floor. Masses of golden birds flew in gigantic curves on the blue carpet under his sad shoes. It must have been autumn because the smell of the flowers and his words are tangled together in my mind.

'Yes. Ah yes. He comes along very nicely . . . the little fellow. You do notice . . . yes . . . progress . . . I feel. I do hope you are being . . .'

His faded eyes twitched as he spoke. His finger picked and picked. Soon, I thought silently, there will be a hole.

'. . . satisfied.' He bent low over her as he spoke the word. She moved her head slightly away from him.

'Oh, yes. Progress. Of a kind, I suppose.'

She waved him away with her hand, and he straightened up. I sat at the piano unmoving. I had developed the technique of listening to a fine art. I could become at will as still and invisible as a chair or a bowl of flowers.

'Such a deal of your talent, Mrs. Moore, has rubbed off on the . . . um . . . little fellow.'

Overcome suddenly by the thought of the stains, he spread his grey long fingers out over the front of his coat, like two very dead starfish on a beach. I played an arpeggio softly and my mother waved her hand towards the door.

'Your train, Mr. Cave. I mean you mustn't miss . . .'

'No. No. Of course not. Well . . .' He paused and looked around the room as if he were trying to memorise it for use during his darker days. 'I'll be on my way so. Time and . . . oh ha . . . trains wait for no man.'

He bowed once more to my mother. She smiled with her lips, but her eyes passed him by. He turned to me.

'And you, young fellamelad . . . till Tuesday. Mind you practise now.'

He moved towards the door. Suddenly I felt some sort of emotion towards him. I no longer remember what it was, and I slipped off the chair and followed him out of the room and across the dark back hall. In the semi-darkness he reached out with a hand and squeezed my shoulder gently.

'Such a beautiful woman, God love her. So . . .' Words failed him.

'What a lucky little fellamelad you are to have a beautiful mammy like that.'

'Have you a coat?'

I pulled with both hands at the brass door-knob and the door came open letting in the east wind. Some letters fluttered on the long mahogany table, and shocked flames twisted for a moment out of the grate and then recovered their equilibrium.

'Coat? No coat, sonny.' He gave a little laugh. 'I never feel the cold.'

A lie, I thought. He was a man, I'd have said, who had never felt warm in his life, or well, or momentarily gay. He stepped bravely out into the evening, and bowed once more before going down the steps.

Father was in the drawing-room when I got back. I stood in the embrasure just outside the door and listened to their voices.

'. . . But go he must. I simply can't bear the thought of having him in the house any more.'

'My dear Alicia, you are absurd.'

'No. Not remotely.'

'But what can I say?'

'An excuse. You must be able to think of something. Anything. He has such an appalling smell.'

'I can hardly say that. Come now.'

I could hear her skirts swish as she moved across the room.

'He must be ill. Some terrible disease. I get the feeling he's leaving it lying around all over the place.'

She opened the window and the wind rattled in.

'He's like someone who's been eaten by life and there's nothing left but this terrible smell . . . More, more air.'

Another window sighed open.

'He's a good teacher. You said so yourself.'

'Frederick, I can't abide him in this house any more. I can't speak more plainly. I shall teach the child myself.'

5

There was a very long silence. My father's face would show little emotion. His voice would show little emotion, but there were times when he would twist his hands together in a gesture of incredible violence. Mother never appeared to notice, or if she did it was of no interest to her.

'Dragging his disease and poverty into my drawing-room. You will write, won't you.' It was a command rather than a question. I heard a quick sigh from father.

'If you insist.'

'Oh but I do.'

The piano teacher never appeared again. My mother became bored or exasperated quite soon by the clumsiness of my fingers and after a while the piano lessons ceased.

It must have been when I was about twelve that the question of my going to school arose, arose that is, as far as I was aware. The dining-room in the daytime was unwelcoming. It faced north and that cold light lay on the walls and furniture without kindness. Luncheon was the only meal I ate with them. Breakfast and high tea I munched alone in the schoolroom. At least I could read, or scribble into my exercise book the prep that I hadn't finished at the regulation prep time. I never minded being alone. I suppose now that I come to think of it I had never known anything else. Even with them I was alone, and I was the only thing that made them not alone. I don't mean by this that they led enclosed lives. To the contrary, they were excellent, generous hosts, and presumably lively guests, but when that side of their lives was quiescent they each retreated into some kind of wilderness of their own. Their only meeting place was the child.

Lunch, that day, was almost over. The cheese and what must have been almost the last of the celery were on the table. I could see through the window the rippling daffodils barely open under the chestnut trees beyond the avenue. A mare with a foal at her tail neatly cropped the spring grass.

'How would you like to go to school then, child, Alexander, hey?'

The question took me completely by surprise, but anyway

6

my mother answered for me.

'Frederick.' Her voice had a warning in it.

He smiled briefly in her direction. A smile that could hardly have reached her down the length of the dining-table.

'Hey then, my boy?'

'I hadn't really thought about it, father.'

'Well think about it. Now's the time. Meet a few chaps of your own age. Broaden. Polish you up a bit. Games,' he said without any enormous conviction. 'Pass the celery please. And things.'

I passed him the celery.

'Mr. Bingham is more than adequate.' Her voice was north-north-east cold.

'Perhaps a widening of outlook would do no harm. There are other subjects which Mr. Bingham . . .'

'He is delicate, Frederick. You must not put his health at risk.'

'In your eyes he is delicate, my dear. I see few signs of it. He has just eaten a most remarkable lunch.'

'Dr. Desmond . . .'

'Dr. Desmond is an ass.'

'Frederick, pas devant . . .'

'My dear good woman, you know perfectly well that Dr. Desmond will say anything you want him to say.'

'You make the most absurd remarks.'

I watched the daffodils and kept my mouth shut. Their words rolled past me up and down the polished length of the table. Their conversations were always the same, like some terrible game, except that unlike normal games, the winner was always the same. They never raised their voices, the words dropped malevolent and cool from their well-bred mouths. Green ringlets of apple peel fell from my mother's fingers on to her plate.

'We agreed on this a long time ago. You remember. You remember very well. Perfectly. The time the child had pneumonia.'

'The situation has changed.'

'Never. It will never change.'

She placed a sliver of apple in her mouth and snapped it shut. Father sighed and folded his napkin carefully along the creases.

'Mr. Bingham is charming,' said mother.

'His charm is not in question.'

'I have no intention of remaining alone in this house with you. I have already said that. Made myself quite clear, I thought. Perhaps you didn't believe me.'

'I suppose I believed you. I almost always do. It was a long time ago.'

'I reiterate.'

'Quite so.'

I must have moved, breathed too deeply or something. His eye fell on me.

'You may be excused, Alexander.'

'Thank you.'

I got down from my chair and left the room. I could feel their eyes watching me as I crossed the miles of floor.

So I missed the formalities of education, whatever good they might have done me. Equipped me better perhaps for the situation I now find myself in? I doubt it. Mr. Bingham taught me the basic facts, whatever other knowledge I have inside my skull I have acquired myself. I will admit to being rather short on team spirit.

Jerry was around always. The stable-yard was where he was always to be seen. He had a neat facility for keeping out of the way of the horses' hooves and the fists of the more quick-tempered men. I noticed his feet before his face. In the summer they were bare, dust-grey and with soles obviously as hard and impervious to stones, thorns, damp, as were the soles of my expensive black leather shoes. In the winter he moved awkwardly in a pair of men's boots tied on to him with string. We never spoke, barely even nodded, and yet I knew that he wasn't just there for the horses, he was as aware of me as he was of their polished perfection.

The lake lay slightly below and to the south of the house.

In the summer it was hidden from the ground-floor windows by the thick leafiness of the shrubs and trees beyond the lawns. In the winter you were always conscious of the grey moving water, which changed sometimes in a matter of minutes to dazzling silver, or blue with tiny frothing waves, endlessly rippling and pushing at the rushes. Beyond, the bog stretched up to the stony peaks of the hills which protected us from the world. They too, like Jerry's feet, underwent their seasonal changes, from the golden whin-flowered gaiety of the spring to the black and dun of clear winter days with the shine of water lying after the rain had passed. Some mornings when I looked out of my window the hills seemed so close that I only had to stretch a hand out beyond the glass to touch them, other days they were unsubstantial, pale, almost in another world. Had I been able to get there by candlelight I would most certainly never have got back again sir. The swans floated for nine months of the year to and fro on the water, sometimes taking off with a great cracking of their wings, then, overcome with the energy they had used up, they would allow themselves to drift on the wind like huge crumpled pieces of paper hurled up in to the sky. Mother's daily ritual was to stroll down the gravelled path to the lake after tea to feed them. They would eat from her fingers light yellow sponge cake, or paper-thin bread and butter broken into small pieces, remnants from the tea table. Occasionally they would heave themselves out of the water and follow her up the path, displacing the neatly raked gravel with their ungainly feet. She would turn and wave them away, clapping her hands softly together, to admonish rather than to alarm.

'The earth is not your element, my loves. Go now. Shooshy, go.'

I heard her call once to them in a voice so unlike her own recognisable voice that for a moment I felt a glow of love for her.

This path of my mother's was not the only one by the lake. In the darkness beneath the trees there were cool green ways that led down towards the village and away beyond it towards the bog and hills. Here, if you were not discovered, it was imperative to take off your shoes, for only in the driest of summers did the paths dry up enough not to leave heavy grey traces of mud on your shoes. I would tuck my socks into my shoes and put them neatly under a bush. Then, in I would go under the low moss-encrusted branches, looking back for the first few moments in case I would be seen, and then become joyfully lost for ever in the dank fly-humming dark. There was an opening by a willow tree where the path became soft grass and slipped down to the water's edge. Here I could swim without being seen. Because of my supposedly tender health I was not allowed to swim except on the hottest days of high summer when the gravel on mother's path burnt its way through the soles of my light summer shoes.

It was about early May when we spoke first. The daffodils were crumpling and shrinking. The weather had been warm and there had been a great surge of leaf growth, the chestnut candles were at their best. I stepped on to the grass from the darkness. There was a sudden noise from under the willow and a splash. My heart thudded with alarm. Down all the years I had been warned about gipsies. I moved with caution across the grass, now long enough to bend caressingly under my feet. At the foot of the tree was a pile of clothes. There was no other sign of life, no sound. I picked up the clothes and hid them away under a bush, then went to the edge of the water to wait for the trespasser.

'Come on in, why don't you?'

A voice shouted from quite far out in the lake. He started to swim towards me and I recognised the shining, grinning face to be Jerry.

I waited until he was standing waist-deep in water just below me before speaking.

'Don't you know this is private property?'

He spat into the water. It wasn't aggressive in any way, merely contemptuous. The blob of spit floated slowly away.

'You're trespassing.'

'Well?'

'I could have you prosecuted.'

'Well, why don't you?'

I felt somewhat foolish. He looked at me for a long time with clear, bright blue eyes rimmed with pink. He had perhaps been staying up too late or possibly crying. I didn't think he looked like someone who cried.

'There's lots of room for both of us,' he said finally. 'Come on in.'

I pondered. He turned away and dived under the water. When he came up he was about twenty yards out. He waved at me. Sparks of water flew from his arm. I took off my clothes and slid down the grass into the water.

It was more fun swimming with someone else, there was no doubt about that. It was not yet warm enough to stay in long. We clambered out on to the grass and stood looking at each other. I had never seen a naked person before. He was much smaller than I was, with twig-like bones that seemed to want to burst out in various places from under the white skin. His legs were slightly bowed. Hair was just starting to grow on his body, in the same sort of lackadaisical way as on my own.

A small wind stirred the leaves and touched the wet skin on my back. Cast ne'er a clout till May be out. I heard the warning voice in my ear. I shivered and then began to laugh.

'I have your clothes. I've hidden them.'

'Where?'

'I won't tell you.'

'I'll make you so.'

'Never. I'm bigger than you. Look. By about a mile.'

I pranced a few steps in front of him.

'That never worried me.'

'You're only a midget.'

'Midget or no . . .'

He threw himself at my legs and we both fell to the ground. He was far stronger than I was and far more agile.

'Midget, is it? Is it? Is it.'

He was pressing my face into the grass. I shook my head and he relaxed his grip a bit.

11

'Say— you're a giant and a hero.'

'You're a damn giant and hero.'

'The biggest, greatest giant and hero in the world.'

'The biggest bloodiest greatest damnedest giant and hellishest hero in the world.'

He laughed.

'And you've the biggest mouth for talking. Will I fill it with grass? Like a hee haw donkey? A wee ass?'

He scrabbled at the grass with one hand.

'Pax.'

'What's that in the name of Jay?'

'Peace. I give in. You win. I'm your humble slave.'

'Where are my clothes, slave?'

'Under that rhododendron.'

He got off my back and threw himself down on the grass.

'You get them, slave, from under the whatchacallit.'

I started to get up but he took hold of my ankle and pulled me down again.

'Ah, forget it.'

We lay staring up at the sun, something I had always been forbidden to do. Danger of blindness, madness, sunstroke, or mysterious things called tumours of the brain.

'I always wonder,' he said, 'if you lay in the sun, in your skin, day in, day out for a year would you go black like a nigger. Heard of niggers?'

'Of course I have. I'm not ignorant. Anyway I don't think you would.'

'Any reason why not?'

'They're born black, after all. It's not just cooking that does it. What's your name?'

'Jeremiah.'

'Why?'

'What do you mean why? It's my name so it is.'

'God help us. It's not exactly a typical peasant name.'

He leaned over and pinched my ear.

'Slave.'

'Alexander...'

12

'Don't be crazy. As if I didn't know. It's as bad as mine. I'll call you Alec.'

'No one else does.'

'So much the better. You can call me Jerry. Everyone else does. Bargain?'

'Bargain.'

'I'll teach you to fight. You teach me to ride. Another bargain?'

'Supposing I don't want to learn to fight?'

'Do you not?'

'I wouldn't mind.'

'A bargain so?'

'Right.'

He held out his hand towards me and I clasped it. We lay and looked at the forbidden sun until it moved behind the trees and the wind started to worry us.

I had a friend. A private and secret friend. I never went to his house nor he to mine. We met, either down by the lake, or up on the hill behind the house where I would take my pony in the afternoons when he had finished school. Up there hidden satisfactorily by a ridge of shining granite we built ourselves a riding school. We moved stones and filled in holes to make a track round the whin bushes, and we built half a dozen light jumps. It seemed perfect to us. After his lesson I would let Pharaoh loose to crop what grass he could and we would crouch in the shelter of a stone wall and work at Jerry's homework.

'All I ever seem to do is boring Latin.'

'Ora pro nobis,' chanted Jerry.

'Oh, hardly that. Boring Caesar's boring Gallic wars. Your Holy Roman stuff would make poor Mr. Bingham faint away.'

Jerry jumped to his feet, scattering books and pencils on to the ground. He stretched his arms out in front of him. Below us the valley was green and moist, an army of conifers listened as he sang.

'Sanctus, sanctus, sanctus Dominus Deus Sabaoth. Pleni sunt coeli et terra gloria tua. Hosanna in excelsis.'

Pharaoh put his head over the wall and blew hot breath down into my face.

'Stop. Stop. Poor Mr. Bingham, you're killing him. Aaaaagony.'

'Kyrie eleison . . .'

'That's not Latin you poor ignoramus.'

'It is so.'

'No. No. Poor midget ignoramus. It's a bit of Greek put in to confuse the peasants like you. At least I think it's Greek. It could be Babylonic.'

'Ignoramus yourself. I bet you don't know the date of the Battle of Clontarf.'

I laughed.

'I do. Mr. Bingham is a whizz on Irish history. The tragic-comic history of the Gael is worth pursuing, my boy, so stay awake.' I mimicked, rather well I thought, his buttoned-up voice.

'Does he really talk like that?'

'More so.'

'Oh Jay, great. Strangled by his dog collar.'

'Right.'

Jerry carried round with him a mouth organ, on which he was able to play with great virtuosity. He would squat down to play, with his eyes shut and his cupped hands pressed up against his mouth. His bare toes would wriggle on the ground in a sort of ecstatic dance of their own. He played ballads, both sentimental and revolutionary, and ancient wordless tunes of almost oriental complication. Sometimes I would try to sing the words that he would throw to me out of the corner of his mouth. I learnt a lot of history that might have alarmed Mr. Bingham. Most times I would just lie in content and listen. When we fought he always won, though as time went on I became a more practical fighter than I had been before. I learnt some tricks, short cuts. On horseback I had the edge

14

over him as far as style was concerned. My style was almost impeccable, his, non-existent, nor did he appreciate the need for such a nicety. But, style or no style, he had no trouble in making my Pharaoh go. Looking back it all seems idyllic, but I'm sure that we had our ugly moments as well as our beautiful ones. Real friendship admits recognition of the ugly as well as the beautiful. I remember the moments that snatched me from the passive solitude of my normal life, warned me of the pleasure and the fear of living.

'I'll be leaving school in June.'

We were lying on top of a hill watching a man and his horse ploughing a long strip of a field below us. The horse's head drooped forward as if it were completely relaxed, its huge white feathered hooves never lost their rhythm for a moment. The man was smoking a pipe and a streamer of smoke trailed behind him as he moved. The perfection of the deep straight lines spread.

'Why?'

'What do you mean why, you omadhán? Because I have to.'

I turned my eyes from the ploughers and looked at Jerry.

'But you're only the same age as I am. I mean a child. We're children yet.'

He punched me on the side of the head.

'I'll not be a child much longer. Then you'll have to watch your step when you're with me, and your lip.'

'What'll you do?'

He nodded down towards the man with the horse.

'That, I suppose. Find some eejit to employ me. There's nothing to do at home but plant the spuds and then dig them up and eat them. I've been doing that for years anyroad. She milks the cow.' He pondered for a moment or two. 'I might run away with the tinkers.'

He didn't sound as if he meant it so I paid no attention to

what sounded to me like a most romantic notion.

'She wants me to join the army.' He spat, as always, un-nervingly close to me. I twitched rather than moved my leg. 'Follow me dad. Then she'd have two envelopes arriving. On the pig's bloody back.'

'You could play your mouth organ in the army band.'

'Thanks a lot. I'd rather stay at home. I don't feel I'm cut out to be a soldier. Perhaps I love myself too much.'

'Look, Jerry . . .'

'Mmmm.'

He was pulling a grass stalk in and out of a gap between his two front teeth.

'Why don't you try and get a job here? In the stables. You'd like that, wouldn't you?'

He shook his head.

'It passed through my mind.'

'But why not? It seems like a great idea to me.'

'Well, for one thing we wouldn't be able to be friends any more.'

Small brisk cries came up from the man ploughing. The horse moved faster, his head now straining forward.

'I don't see that.'

I'd be working for you. It would be different.'

'Not for me, you blithering idiot.'

'Your father, you. It's all one. They wouldn't let us be friends.'

'Why should they care?'

Yet I knew they would care. He was right. My mother's mouth would purse up with disapproval, her voice rise alarm-ingly as it sometimes did when she spoke to my father.

'Why is neither here nor there. Your lot would care. My lot too if it came to it. One's as bad as the other.'

I turned over and lay on my back, looking up at the spring-pale sky. A bank of clouds was edging up from behind the hill, grey and menacing with silver round the edges. A scurrying west wind moved the whins. It would rain before evening. The man below must have got the message also, his voice rose

16

yet again, cajoling, threatening.

'I think when I grow up I'll be a breeder and trainer.'

He didn't say a word.

'I thought that's what I'd really like to do. I'd probably have to go away for a bit and learn something about it, but it's what I'd like to do.'

'Hup, hup, hup, hey,' came up the hill.

'I think about it a lot, and I've never thought of anything I'd like more. I don't think my father would mind. We could be partners. You and I. We could.'

He laughed. I looked over at him. His face never changed colour, winter, spring, summer, it remained pale and peppered under the eyes and on the bridge of his nose with tiny freckles.

'You're a great one for thinking things will be easy.'

'Well? Why not?'

He sighed.

'Ah, you know.'

'We could have a great time. Do you like the idea?'

'I like it fine.'

'That's fixed then. It's good to have the future fixed.'

He grinned. He was undoubtedly wiser than I.

He went, when the time came, to work for one of the local farmers, a tenant of my father, and we were able to meet less often. My life didn't seem to change at all. I grew. At times I was growing so fast that I imagined as I lay in bed at night that I could actually feel myself stretching between the smooth sheets. When it came to growing I left Jerry in the halfpenny place. His finger-nails became engrained with mud and he took to smoking. He would get strands of tobacco stuck on his tongue and would pinch them off between his thumb and forefinger with a gesture I had seen men in the yard use. It put years on his age, or so I thought. Like he had said, he no longer seemed to be a child. He earned the amazing sum of seven shillings and sixpence a week. In spite of the fact that his mother took all but a shilling of it, no Rothschild could have ever enjoyed their money more. We would crouch for hours over the racing page in the paper and with enormous pleasure win and lose hypothetical fortunes. We were the experts, we felt, on form, not only as far as the horses were concerned, the gees, as we called them, but the jockeys also. There was nothing we didn't know about the effects of sudden rainstorms on distant local racecourses or prolonged drought, when legs broke like matchsticks under careless jockeys. Storing up invaluable knowledge for the more affluent future. Jerry's real shillings he spent on cigarettes. I would have the odd puff and cough and he would laugh and look immensely superior and old, old as a tree.

Suddenly he acquired a pony. A crazy-looking skewbald mare, with a white mane and tail.

'It's a tinker pony. I bet you stole it. You'd want to watch out, they'll be after you.'

'Mr. Cleverality, you don't know everything.'

'If you didn't steal it, where did you get it?'

'Her, please. She, her. Mind your manners when you talk about a lady.'

'You damn well pinched her from the tinkers. Lady, my foot.'

He brushed her rump in great sweeping circles with a brush I had temporarily borrowed from the tack room. The pony cropped, completely unperturbed by her new life, at the mountain grass.

'Am I not right?'

'Ask no questions and I'll tell you no lies. One thing I'll say is I'm not likely to go to jail over her.'

'She has very short legs.'

It was the only insult I could think up.

'She'll beat Pharaoh any day.'

'Liar. Rotten midget liar.'

'Want to have a bet on it?'

We christened her Queen Maeve, out of ancient history. We were both satisfied with the name, and he pulled a small bottle out of his pocket and passed it to me.

'Here. We have to drink the babby's health.'

18

'What is it?'

I have always been cautious.

'What do you think? What do people always drink at christenings?'

'Champagne, I believe.'

'That's the quality for you. It's not holy water either. We'll call it champagne though, if that'll make you happy.'

I pulled the cork out and sniffed suspiciously.

'Get on, can't you. It's the real stuff. Man's stuff. It'll make hairs grow on your chest.'

I put the bottle to my mouth and took a delicate sip. Instant tears rushed into my eyes as the liquid scorched down my throat. He took the bottle from my hand and tilted it into his own mouth. I could see through my tears that his reaction was the same as mine. This made me feel a little less foolish. He handed me back the bottle.

'You can have another drop. It leaves no smell. So I've been told anyway . . .'

He rubbed his lower lip with his finger as if it were paining him slightly.

Bravely I took another drink and this time rolled the liquid round inside my mouth for a moment before letting it trickle down my throat.

'What is it?'

'Poteen.'

I nodded. I felt rather pleased.

'Ever hear tell a' that?'

'Of course.'

'Ever had a sup before?'

I considered my chances of getting away with a lie and then shook my head.

'No more have I,' he said. 'It's great stuff.'

'Man's stuff.'

'Yeah, great.'

'Where did you get it?'

He winked.

'That'd be telling.'

19

He took the bottle from me and poured a few drops on to the tips of his fingers. He went over to Queen Maeve.

'It may not be holy water but . . .'

The pony raised her head and he made the sign of the cross between her eyes.

'In nomine patris et filii et spiritus sanctu.'

'Amen.'

'A-a-a-a-amen.'

'I feel Mr. Bingham wouldn't approve.'

'Nor Father McLoughlin neither. Here's to them.'

We finished what was in the bottle, and felt very hot for a while and laughed a lot.

I remember, now that my mind has returned to it, the racing clouds in the pale sky above and, below, the same clouds racing in the water, and it seemed as if we floated between them not connected in any way to the earth. It was my first and best experience of alcohol. Before going home we went down and swam among the clouds in the lake, and sucked in great mouthfuls of them, and sprayed them out all over each other. The sun's golden track across the water made it look, we both agreed, as if walking on the water would be child's play.

Memories slide up to the surface of the mind, like weeds to the surface of the sea, once you begin to stir the depths where every word, every gesture, every sigh lie hidden.

'What will you do with it all?'

There were no leaves on the trees and from where we were I could see the chimneys of the house stretching up towards the grey sky, flags of smoke streaming bravely from them. The lake was in one of its black moods. It heaved uncomfortably and its blackness was broken from time to time by tiny feathers of white, mistakes. We were building some new more challenging jumps, sturdy little stone walls and a couple of brushwood fences. It was cold. My body was warmed by the carrying and stooping, but my hands and face were sting-ing with cold.

'All what?'

'This. Everything. Bloody well everywhere. It'll all be yours.'

'Oh that.'

'Yeah.'

'I haven't thought much about it. I mean, apart from the horses. Are you still on for that?'

'What do you think I am? Some class of a female woman, always changing her mind?'

'You never know with people.'

'If you're still on I am too. Jay, the thought of that day.'

'We'll have to start in a very small way. I've been thinking about that all right. Then it'll be up to you to ride a few winners around the place, well Fairyhouse or somewhere, then people will begin to notice us. You know, think maybe we've got something to offer. We grow from there.'

'You make it sound easy.'

'It'll be easy all right.'

'What if the war comes?'

'War? What war? You do have the strangest notions sometimes.'

'It's spoken of. The Germans are going to fix all those eejits in Europe, the British are going to fix the Germans, and we . . .' He paused for a moment and fumbled in his top pocket for a cigarette butt.

'We . . . ?'

'Oh. We are going to fix the British.'

'Oh, come on now. You dream.'

'That's the talk is in it.'

He ducked his head down out of the wind to light the cigarette.

'Anyway Mr. Bingham says there will be no more wars.'

Jerry spat.

'War,' I said. It didn't seem possible that war could ever touch us within the magic circle of hills.

21

'I'd say Mr. Bingham had a thing or two to learn.'

'He's not too bad really, just a bit of a stick.'

'Does he slam you?'

He passed me the butt, now glowing ferociously.

'He used to pull my ears from time to time, but he doesn't do that any longer. Perhaps I've grown better.'

'Or bigger.'

We laughed. We puffed in turn until the butt couldn't be held any longer, then Jerry stamped it out carefully.

'I'll have to be off. I have the cows to bring in and milk Tooraloo.'

It was discovered. I don't know how, but I had a feeling at the time that Mr. Bingham the ex-ear puller had something to do with it. Maybe it was simply that as time passed we became careless, rode the ponies in view of the house, or laughed too loud at our own bad jokes, whatever it was it came to my mother's ears.

'Is that you, Alexander?'

'Yes, mother.'

'A moment, dear.'

As I crossed the hall I was conscious of my feet clattering ungraciously on the flags. The drawing-room was golden. She sat among the tea things by the fireplace. One of the long windows was open and the smell of newly cut grass was through the room. She got up from her chair as I came in.

'I am going to feed the swans. You may come with me if you like.'

She picked the plate of brown bread up from the tray. A white lace cloth hung in folds almost to the floor. A log sang in the fireplace. I followed her across the room. Her hair and the slipping sun tangled and dazzled together. As we stepped outside on to the terrace she put her warm hand in the crook of my elbow.

22

'The evenings are so beautiful. Ireland should be renamed, I always think, the Island of Evenings. Don't you agree? The perfect time to die. I shall die in the evening, just you wait and see.'

I laughed somewhat feebly. We walked down the steps in silence. She was difficult to talk to, always, either abstracted, or else wanting more than you could give.

'Dead heads,' she said angrily and stopped. She removed her hand from my arm and snapped a dead rose from its stalk. She held it for a moment in her hand looking at it with distaste and then dropped it into my pocket.

'You can dispose of it. Later. That stupid boy has been told too often. Look and look.'

I held my pocket open for two more corpses.

'Apart from looking ugly they stifle growth. There are reasons for everything. This boy seems incapable of learning. Lazy, I suppose.'

She took my arm again and we moved on.

'Careless. No love lost. One always hopes that one will discover the perfect gardener. The potentially perfect gardener.'

'He rakes the paths very nicely.'

'Any fool can rake paths. A machine, if someone invented it, could rake paths. How much time do you spend with that ... ?'

She paused, a long uneasy pause. Her eyes continued to look for dead heads as she spoke. Her fingers on my arm quivered slightly. My heart, even before she finished the sentence, began to thud.

'... person. Child, I suppose I should say. From the village. Don't pretend you don't understand. How much of your time ... ?'

I was blushing violently. I didn't speak.

She removed her hand from my arm and snapped her fingers at me, rather as if I were a dog.

'Alexander?'

'Not much time,' I whispered.

She neither looked at me nor spoke. Holding the plate of

23

bread stiffly before her, a shield of some sort, she moved in front of me. I followed her in silence. The green leaves on each side of us rustled and the rooks were making their usual evening racket. If I were to be born again in another shape I would chose to be a rook. They lead such joyful public lives up there, with their uninhibited screeching and tossing themselves into the sky. They seldom seem to die.

The swans were waiting. One of them was burrowing under a wing with its beak. They heaved themselves ungainly out of the water and stretched their long necks towards us. The hills looked very close and very clear. Rain was in the air. The rushes bowed to her as a little rippling wind stirred through them. A thousand thousand green pikemen bowing.

'With your pikes in good repair,
Says the shan van vocht.'

She looked round at me with disbelief.

'Don't. You never could sing anyway.'

Her fingers crumbled the brown bread angrily, and she held it out. The necks dipped and rose again. The ugly webbed feet squashed the grass. She threw the last pieces into the water and the birds splashed in after them. They were beautiful once more. She took a tiny handkerchief from her pocket and wiped at her fingers.

'What is his name?'

'Jeremiah.'

She laughed.

'M ... mostly he's called Jerry.'

'Well, no more Jerry. No Jeremiah. End to that. Yes.'

She took my arm again and we turned and went back up the path. She walked slowly, leaning slightly on my arm to keep my pace the same as hers.

'You're not really a child any longer. A young man.' She looked up into my face and smiled. 'But of course you must know this without my telling you.'

Her dress was the palest grey and curled out from her legs as she moved them. I wondered irrelevantly what her legs

24

looked like.

'We thought it was time for a little broadening of your education. Mr. Bingham has perhaps served his purpose. I think the time has come when . . . well, I must admit I have always wanted to travel.'

I felt her eyes watching me carefully. I watched my feet as they moved automatically back and forth displacing the gravel.

'This is when real education starts. No more classrooms. You are old enough now to be a good companion. To take good care of me. I thought we might start with Greece.'

'We? You and I?'

'Darling, yes. Don't sound so alarmed. You and I. Why not?'

'Greece.'

'So beautiful, they say. The cradle of . . . Mr. Bingham can tell . . .'

'Yes.'

'Well?'

'Well what?'

'You are being obtuse. Almost like your father. Don't you think it's a perfectly splendid idea?'

Her fingers bit into my arm, like angry little teeth.

'It's all arranged.'

'Supposing I said I didn't want to go?'

'But you won't, will you?'

Her fingers relaxed on my arm.

'No. I don't suppose I will.'

She caressed my cheek briefly with a finger.

'That's settled then. I'm glad. And you won't go off looking for that boy down the village any more. Will you?'

I didn't say anything.

'You won't. It just won't do, darling. It's not . . . well, comme il faut. I forbid it. Absolutely.'

The rest of our walk was in silence . . . At the bottom of the steps she turned to me, the bread plate outstretched.

'Take it to the pantry, there's a good boy.'

I took it from her and ran.

That evening after dinner I was called into the drawing-room. My father always sat in the same chair. It was dark green velvet with a high curved back. It was the sort of chair that, no doubt, his father had sat in before him, and his before him. Generations of male bottoms had hollowed and warmed the seat agreeably. I thought of myself, next in the line. He was working at his pipe. When he wasn't reading or working on farm matters he was working at his pipe. It meant that he was never able to give whatever conversation was going on around him his undivided attention. My mother sat at the piano as if she were about to play. She gently massaged the back of one hand and then the other.

'Ah,' said my father as I entered. He didn't look up from his pipe.

'Do sit down,' suggested my mother, as if I were a stranger. I crossed the room and sat down. The windows were open still and the curtains back. There was still a touch of colour in the sky. Even inside the room I could hear the thin screech of the bats as they swooped down almost to the ground, attracted and alarmed by the light from the room.

'Have a glass of port?'

He was scraping furiously at something inside the bowl of the pipe with a small silver stick.

I blushed and shook my head.

'Lonely, eh?'

'Oh no, father. At least I don't think so.'

'Good, good. Good.'

Mother began to play softly. I don't remember what it was she played, but it was probably Chopin. She was always very keen on Chopin.

'We think it's time you stretched your wings a bit.'

He blew into the stem and frowned.

'Saw a bit of the world. You know.'

'So mother said.'

'Ah yes.'

He reached forward and tapped the pipe sharply on the

26

marble mantelpiece.

'You approve?'

'Well . . . I haven't had much . . .'

'Of course he approves, Frederick. Why do you ask such silly questions? What boy of his age wouldn't approve? I mean to say.'

He frowned again into the bowl and continued with the scraping.

'I thought that next season you might give me a hand with the hunt. We could make you whipper-in if you liked.'

'I'd like that. Very much. Thank you.'

'See how you get on.'

'Yes. We'd have to see. I . . .'

'If there's one thing I hate,' he raised his voice so that she could hear him quite clearly, 'it's music in the background when I'm trying to talk.'

She ignored him as he must have known she would.

'A year or so and I'll be needing a joint master. I'm getting on you know, my boy.'

He took a soft leather pouch from his pocket and began to fill the pipe, pressing the strands of tobacco down with the flat balls of his thumbs.

'Perhaps the time has come for us to get to know each other a little. Hey?'

My face was stiff with embarrassment. I nodded.

'I'll have to be showing you what's what around the place one of these days. When you come back that is.'

'I wouldn't mind starting on that right away.'

He looked dubious. He raised his eyes momentarily from the pipe and glanced over towards the piano.

'I think it would be best if you went away for a while.'

'But isn't there going to be a war?'

My mother took her hands off the keys. A low hum lingered in the room for a few moments. Father struck a match and held it to the neatly packed tobacco.

'I mean . . . well if there's going to be a war it doesn't seem quite sensible to be going off round . . . well . . . I don't sup-

27

pose there is . . . I just wondered.'

She laughed. Her laughter was always charming. Father looked at her again over the flickering flame.

'Dear boy, wherever did you get such an extraordinary idea?' The swish of her skirts as she stood up was like the unfolding of waves on the shore.

'There are undoubtedly tensions,' said my father, 'but I've no doubt they will be ironed out.'

'But where do you hear such stupid things? That's what I'd like to know?'

'A quick flare-up perhaps cannot be ruled out completely.'

The tobacco glowed now as he sucked gently inwards. He looked marginally happier. 'International tensions. Yes. Power seekers.' With a quick irritable gesture of his wrist he shook the match into extinction and dropped it in the grate. 'If you're interested I'll see the papers get brought to you after I have finished with them. Then you can explore these things for yourself. I, myself, have very little interest. I seldom find myself lost among the international pages. I find that where I can have no possible influence a terrible lethargy sets in. Sometimes I regret.' He lit another match. 'Here . . .' he gestured with the flickering match. 'We seem so remote, so protected.'

'Oh Frederick, you do become so boring when you talk on about nothing like that. On and on, ad infinitum saying nothing about nothing. To whom do you speak of such things, Alexander? Not the servants?' Her voice rose to a slight gasp at the thought.

'Of course not.'

'Then?' she demanded.

The flame at the bowl of the pipe fluttered like a butterfly at the tip of a flower.

'People. Around.'

She drew her lips together tightly, angrily, before she spoke. 'You mean that boy. That Jeremiah Crowe.'

'Perhaps.'

The match went out. He held it fading in his fingers.

'What does he know about anything?'

'I don't suppose he knows as much as you, but he knows a lot more than I do. About what happens.'

'You are never to see him again. Do you understand?'

'I understand what you're saying, but truly I don't understand why.'

'Then you must accept my judgement . . .'

She reached across me and pulled the bell, an ornate brass handle on the wall by the fireplace.

'But he's nice. We're . . . he's my friend.'

'Frederick.'

He sighed. The charred matchstick dropped from his fingers. 'In a way, my boy, your mother's right. It's an unsuitable relationship.'

'In every way.'

'I wouldn't quite say that. In many ways though. It is a sad fact, boy, that one has to accept young. Yes, young.' He paused and poked at the glowing tobacco with his little finger-nail. 'The responsibilities and limitations of the class into which you are born. They have to be accepted. But then after all, look at the advantages. Once you accept the advantages then the rest follows. Chaos can set in so easily.'

'Nothing. On and on about nothing. Always the same . . .'

The door opened and the parlour-maid came in.

'The curtains, please.'

She went back to the piano, smoothing her skirts under her as she sat down. The girl crossed the room and closed the windows. It was now quite dark outside.

'Pour me a glass of whiskey, young man,' ordered my father. The heavy glass decanters were on a silver tray. He liked his whiskey undiluted. I poured about an inch and a half into the tumbler. The Grande Valse Brillante swirled around us. The maid pulled and smoothed the curtains with long confident strokes of her hands. I put the glass on the table beside my father. He nodded.

'Will that be all, ma'am?'

'Thank you, yes.'

29

Her voice, like the notes that came from under her fingers, was gay. I never had time to grasp her moods before they had changed.

'You never speak with authority,' she said as the door closed. 'You don't ever sound as if you knew what you were talking about. You have always been an ineffective man.'

His hand was trembling as he picked up his glass. He had temporarily laid down his pipe.

'I suppose that's as good a word for me as any.'

'Ineffective and old.'

I put out a hand and touched his knee. It was a brief gesture, as ineffective as one he might have made himself.

'It's whatever you say. I'll do whatever . . .'

He laughed.

'You do what your mother tells you, my boy. That's the way .. Yes.'

He picked up the pipe again and the process recommenced. I felt that they had finished with me. I got up to go. As I crossed the room, mother called after me, 'Promise then?'

'I suppose so.'

'Promise.'

'Very well.'

I stood outside the door for a few moments after I had closed it, to hear what they would have to say to each other. They said nothing.

We went to Europe. We looked at classical antiquities. We listened to music. We examined cool Italian churches and art galleries till my eyes and feet and mind ached. We ate strange and sometimes delicious meals under dim awnings while the sun baked everything in sight. We passed the time of day with people as charming and detached as ourselves. I acquired a whole catalogue of new sounds, new smells, new sensations. I have all that to thank her for.

When we arrived back the trees around the house were

ragged and almost bare. My mother shivered as she climbed from the motor, I felt nothing but the joy of feeling the hollow hills move closer to protect me, the pleasure of damp air on my face discoloured by the unfiltered sun.

'. . . flesh of my flesh
Bone of my bone thou art, and from thy state
Mine never shall be parted, weal or woe.'

So much for broadening the mind I thought.

My father had failed a little during our absence, not dulled in any way in mind or face, but he seemed a smaller man than I had remembered. My days were no longer spent with Mr. Bingham, but with my father and his land steward, infinitely preferable. He had bought me a chestnut mare. She quivered all over as I put my hand on her neck in a tentative caress and looked at me with eyes of the most magnificent madness, the like of which I had never seen before.

'Ah,' was all I could say.

'Yes,' agreed Paddy the groom. 'A queer price the master paid for her, but he was right.'

'Ah.'

I decided on the spot to call her Morrigan.

'What a strange and very ugly name,' said my mother as we sat at dinner that night.

'The wine, please?'

I passed it to him and I remember his hand shook as he took the bottle from me.

'Did you invent it or have you heard it somewhere?'

'She was a very famous witch.'

'Really, darling, how interesting. Like Morgan le Fay?'

'Something like that.'

'An Irish witch, no doubt, with an extraordinary name like that.'

'She was a great one for changing herself into other shapes. I decided this is her most recent magicking . . .'

'You are absurd.'

'Have you looked at her eyes?' I turned to my father.

31

He smiled.

'I take it you're pleased.'

'As pleased as I have ever been with anything.'

'Good, my boy, good.'

'You astound me, both of you. The child and I spend four months in Europe, and what do either of you care? You'd prefer to discuss a horse's eyes.'

'What would you prefer we discussed?'

She looked at him with contempt and said nothing. I blushed and looked down, away from them, at the smooth glowing silver neatly ordered around my plate. A griffin raised its talon in an angry gesture on the handle of each spoon and fork.

'I am not as uncultivated as you appear to believe.'

His voice was cold, rather uninterested, he was merely making a passing point. After that her silence filled the room as my father and I carried on some sort of forgettable conversation, our words constrained, groping their way as if fogbound from one speaker to the other.

Autumn became winter. Bare trees stretched sideways round the drab garden. The earth was brown and almost luminous with lying water. The mountains were merely a darker grey than the clouds.

Father was a man of method. Each Friday the steward came to his study, his boots carefully wiped, his hat abandoned for a couple of hours on the hall table among the salvers and the flowers and the unopened letters. The estate and house accounts, the rent books and wages sheets were laid out in piles on the desk. My father sat neatly in his chair, the hand that held the pen trembling slightly from time to time. He never smoked his pipe during these sessions, reaching for it with relief only as the steward rose to go.

'You are beginning to understand, I hope, my boy. Figures and papers may seem pointless, but you have to learn to control them. Keep them there.'

He pushed the ball of his thumb down flat on the desk as if he were squashing an insect.

'In this country the land is our most important asset. Yes. Hmmmm. Never be unkind to it. Never skimp. Never treat it with contempt. To be practical, rather than emotional, which I must admit I tend sometimes to be, the more you put into the land the more ultimately you will be able to take out. Like, I suppose, living. Life can be very barren, my boy. Never forget that in these parts the earth is far from barren. Generous. Ah. Your mother has always said that I am a peasant at heart. She's probably right. It doesn't shame me in the least. We all spring from some extinct tribe. To watch your crops grow, your cattle fatten . . .' he laughed, for a moment embarrassed . . . 'Forgive me. It is a simple pleasure, but the greatest one that I have ever known. I am old. I can only speak about what I know. You need not pay any attention. Whoever does? To love the land is more rewarding than any . . . I haven't learnt much. Where my pleasure lies. My faith. Foolish, I probably seem to you. Some people, on the other hand, learn nothing. Nothing at all.'

He always spoke in short sentences, pausing frequently to poke at his pipe, or watch the flame creep along a match held delicately between finger and thumb. Sometimes he would shut his eyes as the words came stuttering from his mouth as if he could no longer bear to look at the world around him. I would listen in almost total silence, weeding what I could for my own use from the tangle of thoughts, memories, dreams and flights of fancy which he was pleased to offer. I think, looking back on it, that he must have spent a certain amount of the time in pain. He had a way of stretching his back suddenly and his neck would become very long and thin, his head would shake for a moment and at the same time his hand would feel cautiously at his back, his fingers exploring the bottom of his thin ribs. I suppose I was afraid to ask him in case he told me something that neither of us wanted to hear. All in all he seemed glad of my company, but in the same sort of way that a man on a desert island must be glad to see and talk to his own shadow from time to time.

I didn't see Jerry at close quarters until the winter was over.

33

The local point-to-point was held one brilliant, freezing spring day. An east wind drove huge shining clouds across the sky and bent the hedges, just beginning to be tipped with green. Jerry and Queen Maeve won a race. In the paddock my father presented him with his prize and shook him by the hand. There was polite clapping from the ladies and gentlemen standing round, and a wild cheer from outside the fence. The pony's neck was black with sweat, and a cloud of sweet-smelling steam rose from her. I held out my hand. Jerry took it without looking at me.

'Congratulations, Jerry.'

His hand was ice-cold. He didn't seem to have grown at all, but looked like a man. I blushed as I recognised an old pair of my breeches on him.

'Thank you.' He muttered. 'Sir.'

'You rode a great race.'

He said nothing.

'She's turned into a splendid little jumper. I always said she would, given half a chance.'

He half-smiled.

'She's not a patch on your new mare.'

'You've seen her.'

'Oh Jay. Haven't I seen her!'

'What do you think of her?'

'She'd take the sight out of your eyes.'

I put my hand out to him again.

'Jerry . . .'

Mother's hand was on my arm. Hard compelling fingers.

'Alexander dear, we must be going. Someone will have to take me home. I find this terrible wind too much to bear.'

She nodded briefly towards Jerry and then pulled me away. Her face was white with both cold and anger.

'I am most displeased.'

She said nothing else until I had helped her into the motor and wrapped a rug around her legs.

'I believe that young man to be involved in some way with some criminal organisation.'

34

'Who?'

'That boy with whom you were carrying on a conversation. You know quite well.'

'What rot.'

'I beg your pardon?'

'I'm sorry, mother, but it really sounds like nonsense.'

'You never can tell what those sort of people will get up to.'

'Jerry's not stupid and he's not a criminal. I don't really know what you mean anyway.'

'There is dangerous disaffection in some places.'

I laughed.

'How old-fashioned you make it sound.'

'I won't have you see with him. Parlons d'autres choses.'

'He rides well. You must give him credit for that.'

'Autres choses, my dear, autres choses.'

Maybe I have been unfair to my mother. I have never been able to understand her motives, which makes it difficult to see people clearly. I have never known any other women, so I cannot measure her up against others of her sex. She had a contrived radiance which strangers took for reality, but which to me seemed to be a thin shell covering some black burning rage which constantly consumed her. When she played the piano she played with an anger that made me uneasy, made me have to leave the room out of some kind of fear, listen from a safe distance. I think she loved me, but wanted for me something about which I had no comprehension. It angered her more and more as the months passed, to watch the mutual pleasure given and received between my father and myself.

We paid very little attention to the war when it happened first. Belgium and Flanders seemed so far away from us. Our fields were gold and firm under our feet. Autumn began to stroke the evening air with frost. Smoke from bonfires was the only smoke to sting our eyes. Cubbing began in the early mornings, the earth temporarily white with mist and dew. A few familiar faces disappeared. War was on the front pages of the newspapers daily brought from Dublin on the train.

'. . . it would be a disgrace for ever to our country, and a

35

reproach to her manhood, and a denial of the lessons of her history, if young Ireland confined her efforts to remain at home to defend the shores of Ireland from an unlikely invasion, and shrank from the duty of proving on the field of battle that gallantry and courage which has distinguished our race through all its history.'

'Damn bloody fools.'

He walked towards the dining-room door, his hands clenched together in front of him. My mother clicked her fingers at me to pick up the paper from the floor. I passed it to her.

'I'm glad to see that Mr. Redmond is behaving at last in a responsible fashion.' She bent forward frowning at the paper catching each word with care.

'Food for cannons.'

He didn't look back towards us as he spoke, merely shouted the three words into the empty hall, and then banged the door behind him. Mother looked at the door with a slight smile on her face and then returned her eyes to the paper.

He became visibly older after this, and, I suspected, took to drinking rather more than was good for him. He retired almost completely into the mysterious tower of his own head and his eyes became red-rimmed and encrusted with mucus of some sort that he had to keep wiping away furtively with the corner of his handkerchief, an activity almost as energy-consuming as playing with his pipe.

We sat one evening in the drawing-room. It was early in October. A monotonous wind had been blowing all day. The windows rattled and the chimneys moaned. A trickle of smoke escaped from the fireplace from time to time into the room. This always irritated my father. He would pull his handkerchief from his pocket and wipe his eyes and dab impatiently at his nose. The leaves had whirled from the branches all day long and the rook's nests, the only winter decoration, were beginning to be uncovered. We were waiting for mother to appear before we had our sherry. I was being troubled by the poems of Mr. Yeats.

36

'Rose of all Roses, Rose of all the world
You, too, have come where the dim tides are hurled
Upon the wharves of sorrow . . .'

I was conscious as I read of my father passing his handkerchief across his eyes and then waving it furiously at the fire. His evening clothes suddenly seemed to be too big for him. Strangely I had no idea what age he was. His hands now seemed to be made of knotted string.

. . . 'and heard ring
The bell that calls us on; the sweet far thing.
Beauty grown sad with its eternity
Made you of us . . .'

'They must be cleaned,' he muttered. 'Remnants of nests.'
The door opened and mother came in. We both stood up. The thin book of poetry fell to the floor as I rose and lay face downwards, its pages slightly buckled under it. She was pale, her lips pressed tightly together in a thin hard line. My father moved to the tray where the glasses and decanter stood.

'Christopher Boyle has been killed.'
I hear now the silken sound of her dress softly moving as she crossed the room.

Father put the stopper of the decanter down carefully on the tray and stood for a moment in silence.

'Flanders,' she said. 'Some place with an unpronounceable name.' She stretched her hands out towards the fire. Soft lace fell around her hands and diamonds glittered on her fingers. My father picked up the decanter and filled three glasses.

'Damn bloody fools,' was all he said.
'I was there when the telegram came.'
She turned her strangely excited eyes towards me. Father put a glass into her hand.

'Waste.'
We drank our sherry in silence and another ribbon of smoke spiralled up towards the darkness of the ceiling. Suddenly father made an angry gesture with his hand and

knocked from the table beside him a small china figure.

'Oh Frederick, you are clumsy.'

We all looked down at the white and gilt fragments on the floor. They seemed like the fallen petals of a flower.

'I'm sorry.'

She shook her head. It could have meant anything or nothing.

'I'll buy you another one. What was it anyway?'

'No.'

She moved towards the bell.

'Leave it,' he said brusquely. 'Don't bother them. I'll pick it up.'

He stooped slowly and began to pick the pieces from the floor. It had been a shepherd, carrying a lamb gaily over his shoulder, one of a pair. His partner smiled unconcerned from the same table.

'I'll get you another one.'

'You can't. They were French, or something. I don't think I liked them very much anyway. Here.' She handed him the waste-paper basket and he dropped the pieces into it. The stooping must have made him feel dizzy. He straightened up with difficulty and put his hand on the back of his chair for support.

'You're growing old,' she commented. 'I've been noticing lately. Ill perhaps? Shouldn't you see the doctor?'

'There's little the doctor can do about my age, my dear.'

'Or ill.' She spoke the words reflectively, her eyes passing on beyond him to a vase of yellow chrysanthemums against the wall.

'Just age. Stiffness of the bones. I am now constantly aware of my body, which younger men are not. I find it unpleasant but the doctor can't help. No.'

'I notice you take a stick when you go walking.'

He acknowledged this observation with a slight bow.

'You will have to get yourself into shape again.'

She took a quick sip from her glass.

'When Alexander goes to the war you won't have him to rely on as you do now. Lean on.'

Father and I started to laugh. After a moment she joined in. We stood around the fireplace with our glasses in our hands like three happy people laughing. The door opened and the maid stood there.

'Dinner is served, ma'am.'

Some time later she was peeling a pear. Dinner had been eaten in almost total silence. Only when the maids were in the room had any of us tried to make conversation. Unease was in all my bones. Behind me the fire sighed and murmured sweetly like people who love must sigh and murmur. The dining-room always looked better at night with the long velvet curtains released from their silk ropes and pools of candlelight on the table. Comfortable meals and uncomfortable talk are always in my mind when I think of that room. The knife she held was silver, the handle ornately curlicued. I have never liked pears.

'Why did you laugh?'

'I suppose,' said my father, 'because your remark was laughable.'

'If you'll excuse me . . .' I stood up to go.

'Sit down.' Her voice was irritable.

I sat down.

'I wasn't making a joke.'

'Mother . . .'

He interrupted me.

'If you weren't making a joke then like everyone else you have taken leave of your senses.'

'No. Oh no, Frederick. He has to go.'

'Push along the port like a good fellow. It seems to me, Alicia, that yesterday, or thereabouts, you were quite unconscious of the existence of this war . . . No. I beg your pardon, you were indifferent to its existence, and now because some unfortunate, misguided young man has been killed you wish to pack off Alexander. What devil is suddenly possessing

39

you?'

'No devil. As you very well know it is his duty to fight.'

'I know no such thing. Anyway the decision must surely
be his.'

'He has no choice.'

'Here he has a choice. For once the British aren't being
complete fools.'

'A moral duty, if nothing else. Why should all the others
go and he not?'

My father stood up.

'I refuse to argue. I have work to see to, you must excuse
me.' He moved towards the door, speaking as he went in an
agitated voice that I have never heard before.

'Everything that you have ever wanted. Everything, Alicia.
Remember that. Ponder deeply before you take away my son.
No is what I say. No.'

'Dulce et decorum est . . . You are old.'

'Yes, I believe now, I am, but I have never aspired to being
an Englishman. Nor have I such aspirations for my son.'

'Our son.'

'Our son.'

'Mr. Redmond . . .'

'Mr. Redmond is a short-sighted fool.'

'Go and see to your work, old man. You're the one with
the devils, not I.'

He left us. She finished her pear in silence. I hate pears. She
wiped her mouth with her napkin and got up. She came up
behind me and put her arms around my neck, pulling my head
back to rest on her soft warm breast. Her fingers stroked my
hair. She smelt sweet and rich and still young. She pulled the
hair back from my forehead and kissed me.

'My boy. My dear, dear boy.'

I hated her.

The door of my father's study was open as I crossed the hall.

'Alexander.'

Mother had gone into the drawing-room. I could hear her
playing the piano.

'Alexander.'

'Coming.'

It was a room full of shadows, a watching room. I had the feeling always that no matter where I stood or sat someone was just behind me, not just wanting the quick conciliatory smile over the shoulder, but someone stern and demanding. Father was sitting by the fire, one hand up in front of his eyes to protect them from the glare of heat from the fire's heart. The other hand held a brandy glass. He nodded to me to sit down. I sat across the fire from him and leaned back into the chair so that the wing was between my face and the flames. For a long time we sat like that, both our vulnerable faces hidden by the darkness. I could hear the breath scratching in his throat and the movement of the fire and the way the living shadows stirred.

'Brandy?' he asked eventually.

'No.'

He raised the glass to his mouth and drank. For a moment the glass chattered against his teeth.

'Perhaps,' he said after a moment, 'the next world makes more sense than this one.'

Somewhere someone sighed. It was not my father, nor was it I. Under the circumstances it was not very comforting.

'Your mother is an admirable woman.'

'Perhaps I will have a drink after all.'

I really said it for something to say. He nodded. I got up and helped myself.

'I lie,' he said.

I sat down again and looked at him. All I could see of his face were his eyes luminous in the darkness.

'I hope you never experience the humiliation of living with someone who is completely indifferent to you. Humiliation.' He paused and took a drink. His other hand fell now into his lap, too tired, it seemed, to defend his eyes any longer. His face was renaissance-carved in trembling gold. I recognised it from my travelling.

'. . . ah . . . yes . . . being unable to touch in any way. For-

41

give me.' He looked over at me. I made some embarrassed, ungracious movement with my head.

'Now I know she hates me, it is better. Strangely. I don't expect you to understand.'

'I'm sure she doesn't . . .' I realised I was interfering.

'Forgive me,' he repeated. 'The heart withers. It is something we must thank God for. You look alarmed.'

'Well . . . I suppose I am in a way.'

'Pour me another drink. You must never feel alarmed when people talk. We have all been too well trained in behaviour. Thank you. My back is giving me trouble tonight.'

'The doctor . . .' I suggested tentatively.

He laughed.

'Why do you say she hates you?'

'You don't think she's packing you off to the war for serious patriotic reasons, do you?'

'I don't know. I won't be going anyway.'

He laughed again. He really seemed to think I was funny.

'Ah, my boy, you'll go all right. You're a coward, so you'll go.'

'More reason to stay, surely?'

'The real cowards are unable to face life, to fear death is mere . . .'

'Riddles,' I said. 'Why do you talk to me in riddles?'

He smiled at me.

'When you come back, that will be the time.'

'They say it will be over by Christmas.'

'Wars tend never to be over by Christmas. Things will change. Here, I mean. I'm not talking about the outside world. Here. If I were a young man . . . I am far too old for commitment. I think that I will probably die soon. I don't mind. I'm not saying it to make you feel pity, or anything. I really don't mind. I would like things to be clear. I would like to know that you will always do what is best for the land. Not for you or her or the strange dreams that may come into your head. Here, the land must come first. You understand. It is this country's heart. It was taken from the people. We . . . I must

42

be clear . . . We took it from the people. I would like to feel that it will, when the moment comes, be handed back in good order.

'I'm not going anywhere, father.'

'We are not totally bad.'

His eyes drooped and jerked open again. I got up and went over and took the glass from his fingers.

'Yes,' he mumbled. 'Yes, please. Then I can sleep.'

'Well . . .'

He banged at my hand with his finger.

'Come on, my boy. No judging, no moralising. Just go ahead and pour me a drink. A large drink. I could get pills from the doctor, but this is more pleasant. Have some more yourself. There's nothing to beat good, old brandy. Probably won't be any left by the time you come back at the rate I'm going through it.'

I took his advice.

'To be a beautiful woman must be a terrible thing. To always expect people to die for you. To always have in front of you the prospect of decay. The wrinkled fingers. Ah yes.'

He smiled almost maliciously at the fire.

'Honestly, father, I don't believe you mean half you say. Words seem to slip uncontrollably out.'

'You might be right, my boy. For years now I've sat here in the evenings working, reading, talking to myself. Till you came along I've had no one to talk to but myself.' He laughed. 'That's a good one . . . till you came along, indeed. I've had some very good conversations with myself about this and that. Yes. This and . . . I suppose I would have talked to her if she had wanted to listen. But why should she? Or anyone? Or you? I haven't acquired the habit of talking with people, only to. You have to feel your way through life. Tap. Tap. Tap. Like a blind man with a stick. I have bored you.'

'No.'

'The wrinkled fingers. One day there will be no one left to die for her and she will be left contemplating her wrinkled . . . I must admit the thought gives me a certain. . . . Go to bed,

43

my boy.'

'And you? Why don't you also?'

'I prefer to stay here for a little while yet. No anxiety is needed.'

I left him sitting there, one hand up again between himself and the fire. No doubt he began to speak to the shadows as soon as I had closed the door.

I suppose if I had had my wits about me I would have gone out there and then into the cool night, but my head was fogged with confusion of thought and brandy. There was no sound from the piano. I presumed she had gone to her room. She would sit by the window brushing her hair with long slow strokes until it began to spark and crackle, then she would lay down the brush and rub her head with the tips of her fingers, working with a circular motion from her forehead up over the crown of her head right down to the nape of her neck. It took time, but she had all the time in the world.

Halfway up the stairs was a high uncurtained window in which I could see as I went up the reflection of the walls, the pictures, the polished banisters, the three antlered heads, the crossed pikes, and a pair of beautifully chased silver swords, the colours distorted by the darkness of the night. The wind drummed for a moment on the panes and fingers of the almost leafless creeper tapped impatiently. The light from the huge glass lantern above the stair-well barely penetrated the passage leading to my room. The embrasures of the bedroom doors were deep and dark like caves. As I reached my room I saw the thin line of light shining beneath the door. She was sitting in the armchair by the fire still dressed as she had been for dinner. She got up as I came into the room.

'What did he say?'

'He was just talking. This and that.'

She walked across the room and pulled back the curtains, then she opened the window. The smell of autumn blew past her, and the sound of a fiddle playing somewhere.

'You're going to become just like him.'

Her voice also was blown back to me by the wind.

44

'Since we came back from Europe I have been seeing this in you all the time. Creeping over you. I had hoped that when you grew up, my darling, I wouldn't have to be lonely any more.'

'I am sorry if I have been inadequate.'

She turned round and looked at me.

'You have been drinking with him.'

'I have.'

'Yes, inadequate would be the word all right.'

She came over and took my hand.

'I don't mean to be unkind. Under other circumstances he would have been a more adequate man. I can't bear to think that you ... You will go, won't you?'

'Mother, I ...'

'It means a lot to me.'

'... don't want to. I really don't feel I have any right to go and shoot people. I mean, for a cause I neither understand nor care about.'

'Right, indeed.'

'Well, yes. I find it hard to express myself.'

'I care. I understand. Isn't that enough?'

I hadn't the nerve to tell her that I didn't believe her.

'I don't feel like being killed either. Or even slightly wounded. It honestly doesn't appeal to me. Really, mother, it doesn't.'

'Why should you be killed? You?'

'Christopher Boyle was.'

'You are a coward.'

'I suppose I must be, if you say so. It's not a very nice word.'

'Cowards are not very nice people.'

'I think if we're not careful we're going to say a lot of things that we'll both regret. I'm not going.'

'Duty? Love? Obedience?'

'No.'

She looked at me intently for a moment without speaking.

'Apart from anything else,' I said, 'father needs me. That is

45

most certainly where my duty lies.'

'Do you think I wanted to stay here all these years? With him? Do you think I'd have stayed if it hadn't been for you?'

'Dear mother, this has got nothing to do with it.'

'Sacrifice. I could have had a life.'

'I'm sorry.'

'Now this one thing I want you to do for me. All the other young men have gone.'

'As father would say . . . fools.'

'Maybe heroes.'

'I shouldn't think so. Anyway isn't it better to have a live coward for a son rather than a dead hero?'

I laughed or tried to.

'You're going to be a cynic, just like him. You grow more and more like him every day. Mannerisms. Turns of phrase. Freakish ways of using your mind. You copy, absorb. Watch and copy. Let me just mention one thing. Suppose he were not your father?' She turned away from me as she spoke the words. Her dress flowed around her like a waterfall. The fire gave her face and hands a beautiful warmth. She looked half frightened, half triumphant, very much alive.

It seemed to take a very long time for her words to reach me, and then to reach right deep into my mind. Hours perhaps. She waited patiently, her hand on the mantelpiece. A knot in a piece of wood exploded and showered the grate and some of the carpet with sparks. Automatically I licked my finger and thumb and stooping down quenched each small red heart quickly.

'Well?'

I looked at the black specks on my thumb.

'Well?'

'I don't suppose you really want me to treat that remark seriously.'

'But I do.'

'Does he know?'

'He knows nothing. Sees nothing.'

I didn't feel as if it were happening to me. I was standing

46

aside watching. Something in my head was banging, an unpleasant feeling about which I could do nothing.

'Who . . . is my father?'

'Oh, he's dead. Long since.' Her voice was casual. It might have been tennis scores she was discussing. 'No need to go into all that. I was very young. You probably won't believe me if I say I barely remember. It was so long ago. Just the orthodox memories spring to mind. Sunshine, sweetness, a lot of laughing. I suppose I was unhappy at some stage. I don't remember. Then I married your father. I was very young.'

'What happened to him?'

'To whom?'

'The man. My . . .'

'He's dead. Like I said. Dead, Alexander. N'en parlons plus.'

'For God's sake, mother . . .'

She put a hand out and touched my shoulder.

'Believe me, it's better not. I haven't made your . . . well . . . Frederick happy, but I did try in the beginning. I tried a bit anyway. I have few illusions about my own character. I'm not a nice woman. I don't suppose I ever would have been, but under other circumstances I might have been . . . oh, I don't know . . . different certainly.'

'You sound so calm about it.'

'Why not. After all I've had a long time to become calm about it.'

'Sleepless night.'

'Oh come, child.'

'I don't mean for you. For me. Dispossessed in a sentence.'

'Don't be melodramatic about it for heaven's sake. Your situation remains unchanged.'

'Not inside my head.'

'That's your affair. You must realise that I would have told you sometime or other.'

She patted my cheek with a patronising hand and then moved towards the door.

'I'm tired.'

47

She stopped with her hand on the knob and turned towards me smiling slightly.

'I do want you to go for all the right reasons as well as a few of the wrong ones.'

She left me. The door sighed behind her. I picked up the poker and beat and beat at the fire. Sparks whirled and fled up the black hole of the chimney, dust and smoke bellowed out of the grate over and around me, fouling my mouth and stinging my eyes. I beat the fire to death and then dropped the poker in the grate and stood trembling and exhausted, utterly alarmed by my own violence. The dust began to settle gradually on the chairs, the bed, the dressing-table, the tall mahogany armoir, the gilt frames on the watercolours. The faded mountain scenes and dim blue lakes became dimmer under the layer of white turf dust. It settled on my evening clothes, and on the pyjamas laid out neatly on my bed. My head began to itch with dust. I brushed somewhat ineffectively at my shoulders. The dust rose, only to settle again. As it settled I felt the withdrawal of all those objects that had been mine by right, under their veil of dust they made their views quite firmly known. She was right, I was being melo-dramatic. I opened the door quietly and went out into the passage, leaving the inanimate, the inimical, behind. Some-where water gurgled down a pipe, there was a shudder and then only the silence of the breathing house. I was glad it was dark. I could escape the eyes of the ancestors on the walls, to whom I was now an intruder. The moon lit the stair-treads with a graceful silver light. The hall door was unlocked. It was never locked. I don't suppose it ever will be locked. In the summer it stands open all day admitting friends and strangers without formality into the high white hall. In the winter it is closed over and friends turn the brass handle and push the door inwards, scraping slightly as it moves over the black and white polished tiles. I pulled it open and went out on to the steps. A fox barked and automatically my mind made a note of the direction from where the sound had come. The fiddler still played. Down the steps and along the avenue the gravel crunched cold under my feet. Drawn by the music I cut off along the path by the lake. The moon had laid a silver way across the black water. There were no lights to be seen on the hills. A very slight frost made my breath curl visibly as it left my mouth. Next year's buds were pale and plump against the glossy leaves of the camellia bushes. I needed God or a friend. I had learnt nothing and there suddenly seemed to be so much I had to know. Through a high narrow gate I went out into the world, just by the crossroads outside the village. The fallen leaves from the trees piled softly by the side of the road.

Eight or ten people were dancing and some more looking on. The fiddler stood by the road's edge, his body moving like a wind-blown branch with each stroke of the bow. From where I stood I could see that he was blind. His eyeballs were criss-crossed with an intricate pattern of veins. They glittered but never moved, saw nothing, had never seen anything. He was old. By his feet lay his long tapping stick and a watchful dog. The music stopped abruptly, and the fiddler stretched his hand out for the bottle that was doing the rounds to be put into it. He took a long drink and then held the bottle out once more until one of the young men took it away from him. His bow scraped harshly on the strings a couple of times and then he threw back his head and began to sing.

'Good men and true in this house who dwell,
To a stranger bouchal I pray you tell
Is the priest at home and may he be seen?
I would speak a word with Father Green.'

Fingers plucked at the sleeve of my coat.
'Is it yourself?'
Jerry was still shaped like a child, small and lath-like, but he was wearing adult clothes too lugubrious for his person-ality. He had a bottle in his hand. He smelt of stale sweat and turf smoke and quite a lot of alcohol.
'I didn't know you were a dancing man.'
'I like a bit of crack. Here.'
He shoved the bottle at me.

49

'No thanks. No. I'd rather not.'

'The priest's at home, boy, and may be seen;
'Tis easy speaking with Father Green;
But you must wait till I go and see
If the holy father alone may be.'

'Ah, for God's sake give it a wipe and have a drink. It'll not kill you.'

I took the white folded handkerchief out of my breast pocket and wiped the lip of the bottle. As he said, it wouldn't kill me. He watched my hands with a certain amusement.

'What is it?'

'Just a drop of the stuff. Don't let the germs worry you, Mr. Alexander, sir. Get it down inside you for old time's sake. Aren't your germs and my germs the one lot of germs anyway? Aren't we breathing the same old germs in and out, in and out in saecula saeculorum. If you remember your Latin like you used to. Sir.' He spat on the ground.

'Well, you've been hard at it anyway.'

With his malicious eyes on me I took rather too large a drink from the bottle. In my mouth the liquid tasted innocuous enough but as I let it down my throat it became a scorching fire rushing into my stomach. I remembered our first experiment.

'Oh God.'

'At the siege of Ross did my father fall,
And at Gorey . . .'

'I'm enlisting tomorrow.'

As he spoke he took the bottle from my hand and then tipped it into his mouth.

'Why on earth . . . ?'

'Cash.'

He wiped his mouth with the back of his hand.

'My dear Jerry, if it was a job you wanted you should have come and asked me.'

He laughed.

50

'What's so funny?'

'Have another drink and you'll see. All in good time you'll see. Let's say to be going on with that the King's shilling stretches further than another man's.'

The burning in the throat was more bearable the second time.

'The hunt . . .'

He shook his head.

'What'll they do without you?'

'They'll manage. Cash.'

He held his hand out in front of him and stared at his empty palm. It was lined like an old man's hand. Paradise for a gipsy.

'Or maybe the thought of all those shiny buttons appeals to me.'

'I thought I'd heard it about that you were with the Shinners . . .'

'Keep your bloody mouth shut.'

He spoke with such violence that my heart thumped against my ribs as if someone had hit me.

'I bear no hate against living thing,
But I love my country above my King.
Now father bless me and let me go
To die if God has ordained it so.'

'Cash, Alec. That's what is driving me.' He smiled and everything was fine. 'You must forgive me. I've had too much to drink, and not yet enough, if you get my meaning. Later on we'll neither of us talk sense and then it won't matter what we say. Here, give me the bottle.'

He drank deep.

'It's the cash.'

'Yes.'

'At Geneva barracks the young man died,
And at Passage they have his body laid.
Good people who live in peace and joy,

51

Give a prayer and a tear for the Croppy Boy.'

He held out his hand to me and I took it. The blind man
scraped the bow twice across the strings and then started up
with a reel.

'Do you want to dance?' I asked him. 'Don't mind me.'

'As you so rightly said yourself, I'm not a dancing man.'

'Let's sit down then. That damn stuff in your bottle has
taken the strength out of my legs.'

We sat down under a tree on the night-damp grass and
watched the moving men and women, the dust rising like
smoke from under their boots as they battered the ground.

'I too, am going tomorrow.'

'What's that?'

All I could see under the tree was the moving gleam of his
eyes.

'To the war.'

He scooped a hollow in the ground between us and propped
the bottle in it.

'Just help yourself when you're dry.'

'We'll go and be heroes together.'

'I don't know how they've got on so long without us.'

'No more do I.'

'They'll turn you into an officer.'

'I don't really care what they do to me. I'm always grateful
for any creature comforts thrown my way. Just as long as I
get out of here.'

'I'm sick of the sight of wet fields.'

'You're not picking the best place to get away from them.
Unless you want to die. Do you want to die?'

'Who in the name of Jay wants to do that?'

'I do.'

'Balls.'

'Have a drink.'

'After you.'

We both had a drink.

'I've been told they hunt in Picardy.'

'Bloody fools, the British.'

'Yes. My mother says I'm not my father's son.'

Jerry scratched the top of his head with a finger.

'So?'

'What do you mean, so? This evening. An hour ago. I am dispossessed.'

'You believed her?'

'Well, yes.'

Jerry laughed.

'What's funny?'

'You're the one they'll make an officer out of.'

'Why would she lie?'

'They all say what suits them. When it suits them. You'll be the same, and I.'

'My ... ah ... father's a good man.'

'Mmm.'

'I'd like to get away without seeing him.'

'You'll feel different in the morning, or, if you have enough of this,' he flicked the bottle with a finger-nail, 'you won't feel anything at all. In fact if you played your cards right you needn't feel anything at all until the bullet hits you.'

'Thanks.'

'You always swam better than I did.'

'Yes.'

'They were great days we had.'

'Yes.'

'Are the swans still there?'

'Yes.'

'Have another drink.'

'After you.'

We both had a drink.

'Why did she say it to you? A thing like that?'

'I don't know.'

'Did you not ask her?'

'I suppose she had reasons of her own.'

'It doesn't matter much one way or the other.'

'It does to me.'

53

'A queer eejit you are.'

'Maybe.'

'There'll be shooting here soon.'

'It'll sort itself out when the war is over.'

'Trained men will come in handy.'

'Jerry . . .'

'Maybe even the likes of you.'

'They've stopped dancing.'

'The blind man's thirsty.'

'Where does he come from?'

'Above in the hills. He walks the road mostly. A bit of begging, a bit of fiddling. They say he's a little wanting. I've never noticed it myself.'

'A travelling man.'

'Nothing on his back bar his coat.'

'No wife?'

I heard him spit.

'You have to promise them the moon or they won't walk down the road behind you. Give it to them and they want the sun. Ever been with a girl?'

I blushed.

'No.'

'No more have I. I have a great curiosity along those lines. And fright. They get you so easy into the palms of their hands. Your mother is a beautiful lady. She used to put me in mind of Helen of Troy.'

'. . . whose beauty summoned Greece to arms,
And drew a thousand ships to Tenedos.'

'Then that day at the point-to-point I was old enough and near enough to see her face and I saw she just wanted the same things, only more of them, as all the other women walking the roads.'

'You talk as if you were older than the hills.'

'Some people are born old and never get any younger.'

'And me?'

'I've never seen any possibility of age in your face.'

54

Chords from the fiddler sounded through the darkness. The laughter of the dancers was soft late-night laughter. Feet shuffled on the road. The trees sighed as if they too longed to join in the dancing. Somewhere someone had lit a fire and the smell of woodsmoke drifted through the air.

He leant over and took hold of my knee. His fingers gripped tightly through the soft cloth. I remember the next morning seeing five little yellow bruises round my knee-cap.

'We'll go together so. Is that right, Alec?'

The world had begun to spin slightly. I had to press my hands hard down on the grass to try and stop everything moving.

'That's right.'

'We'd better drink on it.'

'Yes, we'd better.'

He held the bottle to my lips. The burning had gone out of the liquid, it rushed down my throat like warm water. He pulled the bottle away and drained it.

'And we'll dance.'

He got remarkably quickly to his feet and threw the bottle behind him into the ditch. I got up with difficulty and began to brush the mud and grass from my trousers.

'Why worry?' asked Jerry, reasonably.

Out beyond the trees the moon was shining. It had suddenly turned cold and the earth whirled gently, but not unkindly. Cautiously we moved towards the group around the fiddler, until suddenly we seemed to be sucked into the dance. I was enveloped by the smell of sweat and smoke and drink. Sweating hands brushed my hands, faces whirled and turned, and I too, not knowing what I was doing, or minding, and the earth moved with us all. The whole earth was dancing. The blind man became the author, the mover of every living thing. His face hung above us like the moon, his veined eyes glittering with the power that was in him. As suddenly as the dance had started it stopped. The fiddler stood, bow drooping towards the ground, apparently staring at the sky, hoping for inspiration. I still turned and stumbled through the crowd, half-dancing, half-falling, until I landed on the ground at the blind man's feet.

'Oh God help me,' I heard my own voice call.

From between the legs of the fiddler the dog growled menacingly. Someone behind me laughed derisively.

'Cut it out,' said Jerry roughly.

'Hee hee hee.' The fiddler's laugh was a little mad.

'Da fella's tight.'

'An not the owny wan ayther.'

'Sssh.'

'Or ill is it?'

'Ill, my eye.'

'Sssh, I tell ya, d'ya not see who it is?'

'I couldn't care if it was Charles Stewart Parnell.'

'He's tight, I tell ya.'

'What's so passremarkable in being tight?'

'Cut it out.'

Jerry spoke softly but clearly at them. He stood beside me. The dog continued to growl.

'Hee hee hee.'

Jerry bent down and touched my shoulder. At the sight of the moving hand the dog, whose face was very close to mine, drew back his upper lip in a savage grin. The fiddler let the bow droop until it touched the animal's side. The growling ceased.

'Hee hee. Sez he, God help me. Since when was the blind man God? I had to laugh. Never mind my laughing. God help me, sez he. God help us all, sez I.'

He tucked the fiddle under his chin again and raised his face towards the moon.

'God is up there,' he muttered as he lifted the bow, 'where the cold wind comes from.'

'Come on. Get up before you make a show of yourself.'

He pulled me to my feet. The fiddler was away again. The dancers forgot us. We stumbled our way around them and across the grass to the gate.

'I'm bringing you home.'

56

We held each other's arms as we moved slowly along the path.

'It's home you should be. Tucked up.'

'There's something most important I have to say.'

We stopped for a moment while I thought.

'Well?'

'I can't remember.'

We moved on.

'It's dangerous up here.'

I felt as if the bushes were toppling in on me.

'Closer to the ground . . . ?' suggested Jerry dropping down on to his knees.

'Might be better.'

We crawled until we came to the curved patch of grass between the camellias and the water.

'We must stop. I think I'm drunk.'

'My very own state.'

'I can't go home drunk.'

'I thought gentlemen always went home drunk.'

'What do you know about gentlemen?'

'Little enough.'

'We have one thing in common, Jerry.'

'What's that?'

We both sat side by side on the grass. He put out a hand as he spoke and touched the glossy leaves of the camellia. Next year's buds were nicely formed.

'We both know a good horse when we see one.'

I thought of Morrigan with sentimentality, an emotion that comes with great ease to the truly drunk.

'I really rather liked being a child.'

Jerry laughed. He jumped to his feet and started to pull his clothes off.

'Come on.'

'What are you at?'

'There's only one thing to do.'

He jerked his head towards the lake.

'You're mad.'

'You said you must get home sober.'

57

'But that's crazy.'

'For Jay's sake, Alec, get your clothes off or I'll do it for you.'

I unlaced my evening shoes, like myself the worse for wear, and slowly took off my socks. The grass was unpleasantly cold.

'You've got a queer lot of clothes on.'

Jerry jumped up and down to keep warm, his arms clasped across his narrow chest. I struggled with the buttons of my waistcoat. Soon I was naked too. We looked curiously at each other for a moment and then somewhat self-consciously at the lake.

'Beat you to it.'

He ran across the grass and dived from the bank. As the icy water embraced him completely as no woman ever would, a shower of glittering drops rose and fell, a star-laden wake marked his progress out into the middle of the lake.

'Oh God, that's great!'

Jerry thrust his head and shoulders out of the water and shook the drops from his face.

'I'm sober. Tremendously sober.'

'What did I tell you?'

'Shock treatment.'

'We had great times.'

'We had indeed.'

'Mam used to be all the time down my neck for bathing so much. She always said I'd get my death. If it's not one thing it's another. Germs with you, cold water with her.'

'And my mother thinks if we don't dress for dinner the world'll fall apart.'

'Alec.'

'Mmm.'

'Do you remember the echo?'

'Yes, of course.'

'Race you.'

We swam to the very centre of the lake and turned over and lay on our backs. A million stars seemed to come lower and lower as we stared up at them.

'Echo,' I shouted.

'Cho ... cho ... cho ...'

The sound ran round the line of hills.

'Hello there.'

'O there ... o there ... o there ...'

It sounded like a distant chorus of voices.

'We love you,' shouted Jerry.

'Ove you ... ove you ... ove you ...'

Up at the house a dog began to bark, and his bark was taken up, not by the echo, but by another dog somewhere down the village.

'Bow wow wow wow wow wow', we both barked simultaneously.

'Ow ... ow ... ow ... ow ... ow.' Ghostly dogs answered from the hills. We laughed, and between bursts of laughter barked, and the hills barked and what seemed like all the dogs in the country barked, and we laughed and splashed each other with handfuls of star-silvered water.

'We'll have the whole district awake.' Jerry kicked fountains of sparks up into the air.

'Who cares.'

'We won't be here.'

'No.'

'You won't renege, Alec, will you.'

'What ever gave you that idea.'

'Things may seem different tomorrow.'

'I won't renege. I'm cold. Aren't you? I'm going in. My fingers are dead. I've always suffered from bad circulation.'

Three fingers on each hand were drained of colour and feeling. I began to swim towards the bank, leaving Jerry on his back looking up at the moon. It was almost impossible to believe that the same white face stared down on the trenches, the guns, the barbed wire, the dead.

'Are you not coming in?'

I stood on the bank rubbing at my goose-pimpled body with my shirt and watched him swimming slowly towards me.

Suddenly, as if someone had removed a veil, the sky turned from the deepest blue to early morning grey.

'It's the mud I hate,' complained Jerry arriving at the sloping bank. 'Just the feel of it. A thousand years of duck shit and swan shit oozing through your toes.'

I threw my shirt at him.

'Here, dry yourself with that, there's no point in two shirts being ruined.'

'Thanks.' He caught it and whistled.

'Nice bit of stuff that. Lovely, lovely, too good for the like of me to be drying my body on.'

'Shut up, you damned peasant.'

He threw the shirt around his shoulders and rubbed frantically with his hands. I watched and shivered.

'I feel terrible. Truly terrible. Burning inside, freezing outside. I hate the cold. Draughts. Winter bathrooms, other people's dank passages. Always at this time of year I begin to be filled with nervous apprehension.'

'Well, why don't you get your clothes on instead of standing there gabbing.'

I picked up my vest. It was damp from the grass.

'I'd have thought you'd have been with a girl.'

'Well, I haven't.' I pulled the vest over my head.

'Don't you wonder sometimes?'

'Not much really.'

'I go mad wondering sometimes.' He threw my shirt on to the ground and began to hunt for his clothes.

'Not just wondering in my mind, but every bit of me wonders. You follow?'

'I think so.'

He found his trousers and pulled them on.

'It's no sin. I can tell you that.'

'No, I don't suppose it is. I have never considered it very seriously.'

'I look at my sisters. I know I shouldn't and they'd kill me if they knew, but I can't help it. Do you think that's wrong?'

'I don't know. Honestly, Jerry. I have only a mild curiosity,

60

well contained. I have no sisters, no opportunity anyway.'

'It's handy to have adjacent sisters.' He sighed. 'It seems sad to be going to the war and not to know.'

'Time enough when we come back. They say it'll all be over by Christmas.'

'They say such bloody eejity things.'

A few birds were stirring now. Their sleepy chirping was surprisingly loud. A low mist drifted like smoke just above the surface of the lake.

'The host is riding from Knocknarea
And over the grave of Clooth na Bare;
Caoilte tossing his burning hair,
And Niamh calling Away, come away;
Empty your heart of its mortal dream . . .'

'Is that what you see over there? You look so far away.'

'No. It was only some words came into my head.'

'Your own?'

'Oh God, no. Mr. Yeats.'

'Do you believe in all that? Hosts riding and so on?'

'Yes, in a way. I feel rather stupid saying it though.'

'I'd like to fix that in my mind.' He nodded at the water, the hills gathering themselves for their working day. 'So . . . well . . . like . . . I can bring it out and look at it when I need to.'

'It never works. Haven't you noticed? It's the magic moments when you say—this I will never forget—that go the quickest. I expect all I'll remember is the feeling of my damn wet vest rather than what the lake looks and smells like.' I shivered, shuddered rather, with cold. 'I'm cold, Jerry. The fun's over.'

'Yeah. How does it go on?'

'I can't really remember. Something, something . . .

We come between him and the deed of his hand,
We come between him and the hope of his heart.'

'Oh God,' said Jerry.

I held my hand out towards him.

'We'll meet on the train.'

He touched my bloodless fingers and nodded.

His face, now that the sky was lightening, looked grey, the face of someone already drained by life. It was a very private face, the watchfulness of his eyes was no longer hidden by daytime animation. We stared at each other, then he smiled, or anyway widened his lips.

'I suppose you travel first class.'

'You do have the most incredible pre-conceived ideas.'

'Go on home so and get warm. I'll meet you at the train.'

He laughed suddenly.

'I look forward to seeing the old fella's face when he turns a corner and finds me glaring at him.'

'Why glaring?'

'I've always glared at him. He's rare and quick with the fist, and you need to be always showing him a brave face.'

I left him standing there pointlessly imprisoning the dim hills in his mind.

I have always been surprised at the speed with which the world turns from dark to light. As I went up the path I watched the strip of pink behind the house grow wider and wider. My evening shirt had been new, bought in Rome. Someone would have something to say about that, not to speak of the grass stains on my trousers and the hardening mud on the patent leather shoes. Where the path joined the avenue I stopped and looked at the house and wondered if it would ever be possible to love any person as I loved those blocks of granite, the sleeping windows, the uncompromising greyness, the stern perfection of the building in front of me. My feet crunched on the gravel, almost enough noise to wake the world, but no hand moved a curtain, no face peered down at me.

'Croo,' murmured a pigeon, high up somewhere under the roof.

'Sssh,' I said.

'Croo.'

62

As I turned the brass knob on the hall door my hand left a large muddy smear. I supposed someone would have something to say about that, too.

I lay in bed too long the next morning after the girl had brought in the hot water in a brass can and pulled open the curtains. It was a long time before I dared to open my eyes, and when I did I knew I had been right to keep them closed. The day was far too bright for me, the problem of what you put in your suitcase when you were heading for war was too great to be grappled with. My head swam. I got up eventually and shaved with enormous care. It is essential to shave with care when approaching the major moments. I looked remarkably well and offensively young. I sighed for Jerry's ageless eyes. The gong sounded. Its sonorous note always seemed to proclaim the end of the world rather than the next meal. Outside in the passage a housemaid, somewhat late about her business, was tap-tapping with a broom. Perhaps she too was suffering from the pleasures of the night before.

'Croo, croo croo cuk' said my early-morning friend. He sounded in better shape than I was.

'Damn. Oh God damn. I abhor what I am doing. I abhor myself.'

I tied my tie and wriggled it carefully into position. Mother was always most insistent on an immaculate appearance at the breakfast table. They would be there, immaculate themselves, their heads elegantly bent towards the morning papers and the cream-drenched porridge, starched damask napkins folded neatly across their knees. They would grow old immaculately, their implacable hatred of each other hidden from the world. Is hatred as necessary as love, I wondered, to keep the wheels driving forward? My head ached. I put my coat on and went downstairs.

The table was always covered by a cloth for breakfast. The room as usual had its air of formal gloom. Father was reading the bloodstock sales catalogue and only grunted when I came in. Mother was always surrounded by her own delicacies, a comb of heather honey, her small silver teapot with china tea,

63

the sticky barbados sugar for her porridge, the silver paper knife laid beside her plate each morning with which she opened the envelopes with an elegant twitch of her wrist. She looked up from a letter and smiled.

'Dear boy.'

She held up her face for a kiss. It was as if nothing had changed. I was repelled by the thought of touching her scented skin and walked past her to the hot-plate on the sideboard. I inspected the food under the silver covers, some destined to be eaten, the rest to be thrown to the pigs, and decided that I didn't feel like food. I poured myself a cup of tea and carried it with care to the table and sat down.

I stared out of the window at the garden as there seemed nothing else to do. The grass was still white with last night's dew. A gardener pushing an empty barrow crossed the lawn.

'I hope you're not sulking.'

My mother's voice insinuated itself into my ear like silk into a needle's eye.

'Why should I sulk?'

I knew by the stillness of my father that he was listening.

'I just hoped. That's all. It's too childish to sulk.'

There was a silence. Even though I didn't take sugar I picked up my spoon and stirred my tea.

'Aren't you eating?'

'No.'

'Why not?' There was a touch of anger in her voice.

'I'm not hungry.'

'Are you ill? You usually eat such a good breakfast.'

Her eye lit on an unopened letter in front of her. She picked it up and examined the writing and the post-mark before slitting the top of the envelope. As she extracted the letter she spoke again.

'I do believe you are sulking. You used to sulk as a little boy. An unpleasant habit.'

'I'm not sulking, mother.'

'Then why aren't you eating any breakfast?'

Father stirred uneasily behind his paper. She unfolded the

letter and looked idly at it.

'I've told you, I'm not hungry.'

'It's from Maud.'

She frowned as she read.

'She wants to come and stay for the opening meet. Nonsense.'

'What do you mean nonsense?'

'Of course you're hungry. Young people of your age are always hungry, unless they're ill.'

'I'll never mount Maud again,' said father. 'Not after last time.'

'I can't write and tell her that.'

'Bloody woman needs a camel not a horse.'

'I'll butter you some toast, my darling, and a little of my special honey. It's perfectly delicious this time.'

'How often do I have to say I'm not hungry?'

'He's not hungry,' suggested father from behind the paper.

Mother's mouth tightened ominously.

'The condemned man did not eat a hearty breakfast.' I regretted the rotten joke immediately. Father laid the paper down beside his plate.

'Alexander . . .'

Mother held up her hand.

'We have never had trouble . . .'

'Nor are you having trouble now. I have no ulterior motive in not eating. You don't have to believe me, but it's the truth. Cousin Maud can ride Morrigan.'

Father looked at me as if I were mad.

'For the opening meet? Don't be such a damn fool.'

'As I won't be here I don't see why she shouldn't . . . or you could organise some sort of shuffle round.'

'What do you mean you won't be here?'

'I suppose I will be heading for Belgium by then.'

'There you are,' said mother, 'I told you he was sulking.'

'I see.'

'But, dear boy, you don't have to go before the opening meet.'

65

'Today.'

'Today?' Her voice was shrill and very angry.

'Yes. So if you'll excuse me I'd better . . .'

'Don't you think you're treating us a little unfairly?'

'You confuse me. Last night you said you wanted me to join the army. Today I join the army. I can't see what you're complaining about.'

'You are being extremely insolent.'

'I'm sorry. I don't intend to be. I don't want any more arguments, discussions. I find it impossible to discuss with you. I must just go. I had hoped that you would understand.'

'You don't have to go today.'

'I do. I had thought of just getting up and going. Crack of dawn, something like that, but I thought better of it.'

She gestured helplessly with her hands.

'If you must, you must. Other young men don't carry on with all this . . .'

'I have to catch the Dublin train. I think I should go and pack.'

'. . . fuss.'

In spite of the petulance of her words, I was conscious of a radiance coming from her, a feeling of triumph.

'I think we should send him up in the motor, don't you, Frederick?'

'I would prefer to go by train. I'm afraid I shall have to ask you for some money, father. I'm sorry.'

'By all means.'

He picked up the paper again and retired behind it. His hands were shaking.

Mother dabbed at the corner of her mouth with her napkin, removing all traces of the special honey, the nutty-tasting toast.

'You have been very thoughtless, dear boy, but I will forgive you. Come. Let me do your packing for you.'

She got up and came over to me. She touched my face with a cool finger. I shook it away as I would a fly.

'Let me help you.'

66

'I'm only bringing my tooth-brush.'

'You're so absurd.'

'Yes.' I stood up.

Father blew his nose behind the paper.

'Well,' he said, 'if you've made up your mind to go the quicker you go the better.'

'Quite.'

'Pity about the opening meet.'

'Yes.'

'I'll fix something up for Maud. Pity to let her ride Morrigan. She'll pull the mouth off her. Might even have a stab at her myself.'

'I'd like that.'

'Mmmm.'

He got up abruptly and made for the door.

'Your grandfather was a soldier. I can't say it got him anywhere. I'll be in the study when you're ready. Sure you don't want the motor?'

'Quite sure.'

I listened to his feet crossing the hall. I listened to him open and close the study door.

'I am so proud of you,' my mother said behind me.

I laughed and went upstairs to pack.

I put my tooth-brush and some underclothes into a small brown leather case and then sat on the end of my bed. They would put moth-balls in all the drawers and in the tall mahogany press, and they would forget to open the window, and after a while anonymity would take over. That would be right. If ever I came into the room again I would be a different person. The door opened and father came in. He looked at me for a moment before speaking.

'I have to go out,' he said.

I nodded. He held a bundle of notes out towards me.

'Yes. I have to. Something has come up.'

'That's all right, father.'

'Here. It's all I have about the place, but I'll send you more.'

67

'Thank you.'

I took the money and didn't know what to do with it.

'Don't let yourself go short. Anything you want . . .'

'Thank you.'

'I have to go. I couldn't just sit down there.'

'I know.'

'Your mother will want to say goodbye on her own. I do insist that you are kind to her.'

'Yes.'

'Put that money away boy, you'll lose it.'

I pushed it into my coat pocket.

'It'll be all right.'

He probed in his waistcoat and pulled out his gold watch. 'Sentimentality doesn't suit either of us. Let us call this a traditional gesture. It was my father's. Balaclava and all that nonsense. Take it, take it for God's sake. He was a great horseman. A giant. I've no doubt he was a rotten soldier though. At least he died in his bed. Now it's yours. I don't need a watch these days. The whole house full of damned clocks. Ticking everywhere. Put it away.'

It was warm in my hand with the warmth of his body. I put it into my pocket along with the money.

'Thank you. I'd give Charlie Brennan my coat and let him take over as whip.'

'Brennan?'

'He's as good a man as any.'

'I'll bear him in mind. Well . . . Packed?'

'Just the tooth-brush. No point . . .'

'Quite.'

'It's a pity about the opening meet.'

'Next year.'

I bent down and picked up the case. I held out my hand.

'Goodbye.'

He took it.

'Goodbye, my boy. Don't, ah, indulge in too much foolishness.'

'I'll write.'

'Yes. Forgive me for not coming down.'

'Goodbye.'

I left him standing there.

Mother was standing in the drawing-room waiting for me. She threw out her arms as I came in with a splendidly theatrical gesture. I walked towards her. The room seemed about a mile long. I finally reached her and her hands flew like two birds around my neck and she pulled my face down to hers. I kissed one cheek and then the other. She still held me. I put up my hands and unfastened hers. Her eyes were the most triumphant blue.

'You'll come to see us in your uniform, won't you?'

'Mother, there's just one thing I must say before I go.'

'Yes?'

'About what you said last night.'

She smiled at me.

'Go ahead, darling.'

'I don't believe you. I never will believe you.'

She laughed a little.

'Run along, dear boy, you'll miss your train.'

I turned and went towards the door. The journey was not so long that way. She called after me.

'Write. Do write. I will be so looking forward to your letters.'

In the hall the servants gathered round clutching at my hands and touching my coat. Mrs. Williams the cook cried into a large blue handkerchief. The word had got around quickly. 'I'll see you all at Christmas,' was all I could think of to say and then I ran down the steps and got into the motor. I opened the window so that I could smell the turf smoke and catch a glimpse of the two swans rocking gently on the lake.

How many miles to Babylon?

A strange thought for such a moment.

Four score and ten, sir.

It was the only thing in my mind. The strange bumpy rhyme that I hadn't heard for years.

Will I get there by candlelight?

69

The orange leaves from the chestnut trees danced in front of us all the way down the avenue.

Yes and back again, sir.

The next six weeks were spent on the shores of Belfast Lough learning to be a soldier. It was like some mad children's game, except that the rules had to be taken seriously. Jerry had been right, it never entered their heads that I should be anything but an officer. I grew a moustache in order to give my face a little more authority, to hide my soft childlike mouth, or perhaps merely to raise a smile in myself every time I confronted myself in the glass. Nothing remotely memorable happened until the first of December when Major Glendinning sent for me and told me that I would be leaving for the front with him the next day. He then stared at me for a long time across his polished desk. There seemed nothing to do but stare back. His face appeared to be made of very well cared for leather. His hands could lie still on the desk in front of him as if they were just two more of the inanimate objects that covered the surface. He had a habit of biting off the end of each word with his large shining teeth, as it passed out through his lips. He looked like a man who knew all about self-control.

'It is my lot, Mr. Moore,' he spoke at last, 'to have been landed with the biggest bunch of incompetents I have come across in my life. Illiterate peasants, rascals and schoolboys. However, I intend to make soldiers of you.'

I had heard it before. He had harangued us once a week for all six weeks. I knew better than to speak.

'The best of a bad job. That's all we can do. Parade your men at nine sharp.'

'Yes, sir.'

I didn't know whether I was dismissed or not. He picked one of his hands up from the desk and wrote some words on a piece of paper. Then he looked up at me again, or through me, it felt like.

'You're from Dublin way?'

'Thereabouts, sir.'

'We'll be picking up another couple of incompetents there on our way through. You can have a couple of hours off to see your people if you want.'

'Thank you, sir, but I'd rather not.'

'It's up to you.'

'I'd rather just leave it, sir.'

He wrote something else on the paper.

'You can go.'

'Thank you, sir.'

As I reached the door he called my name.

'Mr. Moore.'

'Sir?'

'Mix.'

'Mix, sir?'

'That's what I said. I watch, you know. I get the impression you think you're better than everyone else.'

'Oh no, sir.'

'Why don't you mix then?'

'I hadn't really thought about it, sir.'

'No?'

'I don't know what to say, sir.'

'The trouble with a war like this is you get the wrong types joining up. Non-starters.'

'I'm sorry, sir, if you're dissatisfied in any way. I'd be quite happy in the ranks.'

'Damn stupid thing to say.'

He tore up the paper in front of him and threw it in the waste-paper basket. I felt he was making some personal comment as he did so.

'Just pull yourself together and mix. You can go. Parade at nine and don't forget what I said.'

Small beads of sweat crept out from under my hair and trickled down my forehead as I shut the door behind me. The N.C.O. on duty grinned at me. I took my handkerchief from my pocket and wiped my forehead. He winked. I nodded at him with what I hoped was dignity.

Jerry was hanging around outside the building. It was the first time I had seen him on his own since we joined up. He saluted. They had cut his hair and spruced him up a little, but he didn't look like a real soldier. We walked along the path towards the mess together.

'Well, Alec?'

'How are things with you?'

He looked around cautiously before spitting.

'We're off tomorrow.'

'I heard tell. Do you think we'll be home for Christmas?'

'Ha ha.'

'Just what I would have said myself.'

'What do you think it'll be like?'

'Alec, me old son, it couldn't be worse than here.'

'Just what I would have said myself.'

'I'd better be off before they court-martial me for hob-nobbing with an officer. So long.'

He shoved his hands deep into his pockets, against all the rules, and jingled some coins.

'Goodbye, Jerry. Good luck.'

He walked away, jingling as he went. It began to rain, large drops that burst as they hit you into a million icy fragments. He began to run, also, I was sure, against the rules. Only run when you are attacking the enemy, and then make sure you are running towards him and not any other damn cowardly inefficient way. At the corner of the building he stopped and turned back towards me. He took his right hand from his pocket and drew it quickly across his throat. A salute of his own invention. Then he was gone. I was getting very wet.

It rained all the next day.

We were joined in Dublin by another hundred men and a couple of subalterns from the third battalion. They looked no great shakes. Poor Glendinning, I thought, how sad for you that we constitute no grave danger to the Hun. Grey crowds lined the grey streets. A few women called God bless you. We were soaked to the skin by the time we reached the boat. She backed, as she had done when I travelled with my mother, out of Kingstown harbour and then turned her stern towards the war.

Even under the low rain clouds the bay was beautiful, ringed by its hills and festooned with pale glittering lights, like jewels. The Bailey light flashed its warning and salutation. Kingstown answered. Gulls mewed above us and wheeled and skimmed the sky-grey sea. How many miles . . . ? Some of the men went on waving until the city was no more than a soft green blur reflected in the clouds.

Our first casualty was some poor fool who cut his wrists before we even landed in England. Apart from that the journey was uneventful. Rules and yet more rules. Each of the men was given a copy of the following directive and told to keep it in his Pay Book and obviously read it in moments of temptation.

'You are ordered abroad as a soldier of the King to help our French comrades against the invasion of a common enemy. You have to perform a task which will need your courage, your energy, your patience. Remember that the honour of the British Army depends on your individual conduct. It will be your duty not only to set an example of discipline and perfect steadiness under fire but also to maintain the most friendly relations with those you are helping in this struggle. In this new experience you may find temptation in both wine and women. You must entirely resist both temptations, and, while treating all women with perfect courtesy, you should avoid any intimacy. Do your duty bravely. Fear God. Honour the King.'

Poor Jerry I thought, my heart bleeds for you.

We landed at Le Havre where, owing to intense confusion about transport, we had to camp for several days. The men complained constantly. The major created more rules. We were ordered not to eat pork when we got up near the front, as the pigs that remained alive, not many I may say, fed and

73

grew temptingly fat on human flesh. English, French, German. The pig is no chauvinist, all races are the same to the curly-tailed pig. The countryside was dismal. We were all permanently wet. Eventually we were packed into a train and then unpacked at Bailleul fairly late in the evening. It was still raining. We marched the last ten miles to West Outre that night along a road cobbled with stones larger than duck eggs and greasy with mud and horse dung. The centre of the road though pitted by the heavy traffic was paradise compared to the edges where we were forced to spend most of our time wading through mud above our ankles and spattered with filth by the constantly passing transport lorries. The men, of course, complained. Our base was, and has remained, a small derelict farm. A wall with a high metal gate shut us in from the road. There were two barns, one on each side of the yard, for the men, and a squat stone farmhouse where Major Glendinning, Bennett and myself, the N.C.O.s, and the orderlies set up house. In the distance we could hear the big guns, and now and then over to our right the sound of musketry fire, rather too close for total comfort. From time to time the ground shook under us and the few remaining windows would rattle in their frames. There was a wild-looking mongrel who padded his way from room to room searching for his masters and stole any food you took your eye off for a moment. He was indifferent to either pats or blows from the men, his only interest left being survival.

Bennett, who seemed a nice enough young man, had joined us at Bailleul. Though he was only a few months older than I was myself and had also only just come over from England he had an air of someone who had seen it all before. He knew the ropes. We shared a small attic, frequently with the dog, who added a pungency to the atmosphere which neither of us enjoyed but equally neither of us had the heart to do anything about. The only window still had its glass, and there was a small fireplace in which our orderly lit a fire daily. It smoked almost unbearably, but at least we were able to keep our clothes dry.

74

On our third morning there the sun was suddenly shining. We went out into the yard and looked at it.

'It's real,' he said.

'There's not much warmth in it.'

'You can't have everything. I know where we could get a couple of horses.'

'Don't be an ass, Bennett, Major Glendinning won't let us go riding.'

'Who's going to tell him?'

'You have a point.'

I thought of Jerry.

'Could you make it three?'

'Why so?'

It was one of his favourite words. Everything was questioned in his cool young English voice. He never really cared what the answer was, it only seemed important to him that he should ask the question.

'I have a friend . . .'

'Righty ho. What fun it'll be.'

He disappeared. I went out of the gate and down the road where some of the men were raising mighty earthworks in the interests of discipline, morale and whiling away the time.

'Could I have Private Crowe for an hour or so?' I asked the N.C.O. in charge.

'You can and welcome.'

He'd never have spoken like that to the Major or indeed Bennett. He turned to the men.

'Crowe, you good for nothing, get your backside out of there at once, Mr. Moore wants you.'

Jerry climbed out of the hole. He saluted. I turned and walked away as fast as I could. I could hear him almost running to keep up with me.

'I have some horses.'

'Jay.'

We went past the gates away from the possible eye of Major Glendinning or the C.S.M. who had no respect for junior officers.

'Real horses.'

'Wait and see.'

'How did you manage?'

'Friends in the right places.'

He spat on the ground. I felt better as I looked at him than I had felt for some time. Bennett rode around the corner at that moment leading a pair of bays.

'Jay. Oh holy Jay.'

'Your friend?' asked Bennett, stopping beside us.

'Jerry Crowe. The best horseman in County Wicklow. No damn style mind you, but nonetheless the best.'

Bennett gravely leant down and held out his hand to Jerry. I liked him from that moment.

'Bennett is my name.'

Jerry shook his hand.

'In the great English tradition,' I said as I mounted, 'he lacks a christian name.'

'Ah, sure we all know the English aren't Christians anyway so I'm not surprised.'

'Hop on and let's away before someone feels they need us to dig even more latrines.'

We followed him along the road. He seemed to know where he was going. We left the road and cut across a field where some peasants were turning the earth over and over with long flat spades. Above the field was a long ridge of hill decorated here and there with sad winter trees. Bennett nodded towards it.

'Want to see a show?'

'A show?'

'Never mind. Come follow follow follow me.'

He put his spurs to the horse and was off up the long slope. The horse beneath me trembled with pleasure. The beautiful smell of his sweat was in my nose. With a grunt Jerry was past me crouched low like a jockey in his saddle. On the firm ground above the fields the whole world was drumming hooves. We swung away to the right and up on to the brow of the hill, then Bennett drew rein. He looked at Jerry and grinned. 'Our friend here is right about your style. You'll never be a gentleman rider, but I'd back you to win any day.'

'I spit on gentlemen riders.'

'Right,' said Bennett. He looked away and down over the plain that stretched beneath us. He thrust his hand out pointing his boney finger.

'My show, gentlemen.'

The sky was immense. Huge white clouds, their bellies stained black by the drifting smoke from the land, floated with dignity across it. Away to the left the cathedral at Ypres pointed accusingly at heaven. Far, far beyond the town on the horizon a line of white charming puff-balls appeared and disintegrated, a background to the grey tormented landscape. Nearer and to the right the big guns were blasting away and grey smoke swirled up to the clouds. Some farmhouses were burning gaily. No living thing moved. By some freak of the wind we could only hear the gentlest rumbling of the guns, not even enough to twitch the horses' ears.

'Jay,' said Jerry.

'Some great show, eh?'

'In an odd way it's almost beautiful.'

'Games.'

'Quite.'

'It's a game I'd rather be watching,' said Jerry.

'I don't know,' Bennett's voice was thoughtful.

We all continued to stare at the changing patterns of smoke and cloud. My horse became impatient and pawed angrily at the ground, shaking his head with a fine jangling of harness. I realised that I was bitterly cold.

'Well, I'd rather watch it than be in it, and I'd rather be home than either.' Jerry sounded as if he meant it.

'Why so?'

'Ah, for Christ's sake!'

'I think there's something rather splendid about it all. There's always the chance that one might become a hero. Doesn't that stir your blood?'

'I can't say that it does.'

77

'I'm cold,' I said to them.

'I take it then that it doesn't stir your blood either.'

He pulled his horse's head round as he spoke and we set off across the hillside.

'Not a movement.'

'And I've been brought up to believe that you Irish were so romantic.'

'There's nothing remotely romantic about all that, least of all the thought that we'll be in at any moment.'

'Pity.'

Jerry spat.

'You know,' said Bennett, 'my life until now has really been indescribably dull. Patterns. Everywhere you look, patterns. This is the best thing that has ever happened to me. I'll either become a hero or I'll die.'

'Death is more permanent,' I suggested.

He laughed.

'The other thing I've always been told about you lot is that you're cynics. Maybe you'll allow that to be true.'

'Maybe.'

'At least death is a mystery.'

'So is tomorrow.'

'What rot, young man, merely a disappointment.'

He looked for a moment at Jerry who had cantered ahead.

'Friends?'

'Yes. Friends.'

'Howso?'

'Don't be such a damn English snob.'

'It appears to me that you attach the adjective English to anything you don't like.'

'Maybe. It comes easily. I suppose we have a lot to learn about each other.'

'You're just another bundle in the White Man's Burden.'

I laughed edgily. Sometimes jokes go too far. Bennett was the sort of man who would always push his luck. The death or heroism streak. Jerry slowed down to a walk and we caught up with him.

'Tell me, Jerry, what did you join up for?'

'The brass.'

Bennett was non-plussed.

'The cash, man, and he,' he jerked his head towards me, 'joined because his Mammy wanted to get rid of him. Now you know it all.' I felt myself blushing. Bennett looked startled. This didn't seem to conform to his known patterns. I began to laugh.

'Are you ... ah ... pulling my leg?'

'Oh God, no. Ask himself there.'

Bennett looked at me.

'True?'

'There is a strong element ... though mind you I don't think I'd have mentioned it myself. Jerry's a contortionist.'

Jerry looked pleased.

'My mother cried. Yes. It wasn't unexpected, but ...'

'Mine played Chopin triumphantly on the piano the moment I left the room,' I invented. It seemed highly likely. 'Grande Valse Brillante.'

'Dum de da da dum dee dada.'

'Exactly.'

'How very remarkable.'

'Candles and novenas,' said Jerry somewhat enigmatically.

'What's that?'

'Mam. Candles and novenas. Decades of the rosary. Bending the ear of poor bloody God. Oh Jay.'

His whole body had become electrified.

'Would ya looka.'

His finger pointed, trembling with excitement, down the hill and across a drain running with thick brown water to a large sloping field beyond. Walking casually across the field as if he had all the time in the world was a fox. A stupid, unsuspecting French fox. We were off, and over the drain like birds lifting from a summer hillside. And it ran. Thank God it ran, and we ran. It must have been a good fifteen minutes before it went to ground in a shell-shattered spinney. Steam rose from the horses, my heart was hammering. The wounded and blackened trees were quite still, practically dead, and gradually the sounds of the war reached our minds again.

'Well, wasn't that great?'

Jerry winked at me as he spoke. I laughed. We all laughed. Bennett pulled a large clean handkerchief from his pocket and blotted at his forehead.

'I think I'll come and live in Ireland when this show is over.'

We walked the horses soberly back over the fields.

'I'll come and live near you and between us we'll teach Jerry to ride like a gentleman.'

'The divil you will.'

'But you're all rolled up like a football, man.'

'And I'll beat you any time so I will.'

'I don't deny that. It's just for appearances, not performance.'

Jerry spat.

'We're thinking of starting a small stud and training stables. Jerry and I. We thought . . .'

'I like the thought. A good good thought.'

'Hey, you.'

A small irate major appeared through a gap in the hedge. What could be seen of his face behind an enormous moustache was mauve with anger.

'Hey, you.'

'Sir,' said Bennett, saluting almost gaily as he drew rein.

'Dismount,' he bawled at us.

He looked us up and down as we stood stiffly to attention.

'What the blazes do you think you're up to?'

He gestured towards the hill with an angry hand. I noticed, irrelevantly, that he wore khaki mittens and only the two top joints of his fingers appeared.

'I've been watching you for the last twenty minutes. Have you taken leave of your senses?'

'We . . . ah . . . found a fox, sir.' I spoke, as neither of the others seemed to want to.

'A fox?'

He stared at me with disbelief. He didn't say anything else for several very long moments. His fingers groped in his breast pocket and pulled out a note-book and pencil. His nails were stained dark brown and hooked slightly over the tops of his fingers. Maybe he had been a bat in former life, though he didn't appear to have any trouble with his eyesight.

'Yes, sir, a fox.'

'Name?'

'Moore, sir.'

'Regiment?'

'Royal Irish Rifles, sir.'

'Agh. Next. You.'

'Bennett, sir. Attached to the Royal Irish Rifles, sir.'

The major wrote busily.

'They apparently have a shortage of junior officers, sir.'

Why the hell, I thought, couldn't he leave well alone? No need to engage the old bastard in needless chit chat.

'Any information I require I shall ask for, thank you, Mr. Bennett. And you?'

'Private Crowe, sir.'

He saluted as he spoke.

'What is this man doing with you?'

'We . . . I mean I invited him to come along.'

'He's . . .' Bennett obviously thought it was better not to finish. The major looked at him with unpleasant politeness.

'Yes, Mr. Bennett?'

'Nothing, sir.'

'You are probably wise.'

He wrote some final words in his book and then shut it with an angry little snap. He put it carefully back in his pocket, tucking the pencil in beside it, smoothing the outside flap down with his fingers.

'I suppose you think you're here for fun.'

'Oh no, sir.' Bennett's voice was really shocked. 'I mean to say . . .'

'Damned schoolboys. Where did you get those horses from anyway?'

'A friend,' said Bennett somewhat vaguely.

The thought crossed my mind that he had in fact stolen them, temporarily of course.

'Exercising . . .'

'Who is your commanding officer?'

'Major Glendinning, sir.'

'Make no mistake about it I will inform him of your behaviour. Of your . . . your . . .' His face became shades darker as he searched for the right word and failed to find it . . . 'behaviour. It will be up to him. Though, mind you, I will recommend . . .' His voice died on him and he looked at us in silence. 'And as for you . . .' His eyes had shifted to Jerry. There was another long silence. 'You may remount,' he said finally. 'Get back to your billets at once.'

We remounted and began to move slowly off.

'Make no damn mistake.' He shouted the words at us as we went through the gap in the hedge into the lane, leaving him alone in the field.

'Trouble,' said Jerry after a moment.

'I suppose one has to pay for one's pleasures,' said Bennett pompously. 'Let's look on the bright side. Maybe the bold major will meet a wandering bullet. After all there's a man killed every minute, why not that nasty little chartered accountant? Why not?'

'I wouldn't wish that on the fella.'

'One mustn't be squeamish about these things.'

It was beginning to rain. The wind was blowing straight in our faces and the drops were like a million needles almost puncturing the skin. We pulled up the collars of our coats and hunched ourselves in the saddles like Jerry in an effort to keep warm. A dead horse lying by the side of the lane, its body swollen by whatever chemical changes were going on inside it, was the only visible sign of violence. The noise of shelling folded and unfolded in the distance. The rhythmic beat of the horses' hooves and the creaking of our saddles were the only noises that I was completely conscious of.

'All right,' said Bennett suddenly, 'let me have the horses.

82

You get on back to the farm as quickly as you can. On down the lane there and you'll come to the road.'

Obediently we dismounted and handed him the reins. He winked.

'A good time was had by all?'

'Splendid.'

'Ask no questions then. I'll see you later.'

He was off, picking his way across a field towards a grove of black trees.

'I bet he pinched them,' said Jerry.

'I've no doubt of it.'

'Great. I like that. You know for an Englishman and all it's not bad.'

We walked down the lane. Soon it would be dark.

'Well, that's another day we've got through anyway.'

'Mmm.'

'Bloody rain,' he said.

'Mmmm.'

'Bloody country.'

'Mmmm.'

'Bloody war.'

'Mmmm.'

The next morning we went up to the front line.

The system was that we spent three days in the front trenches and then withdrew to the support trenches for three days and then back to the front again. After about two weeks we went back to the farm for five or six days rest, and so on. At that time we were in no serious danger in the front trenches as the Huns' artillery and ours were whamming shells at each other over our heads. Snipers were our main problem as the parapet was in some places only about three feet high and to allow your head to appear for even a moment over the top was asking for trouble. In the support trenches there was always the chance that a mis-aimed shell from the enemy might blow us all to smithereens at any moment. The shells would land behind us blowing great fountains of earth, stones, branches, fragmented bodies of animals and men high

83

into the air, and we would be disagreeably peppered with falling debris. Most of our time was spent repairing and extending the trenches and rebuilding the parapets, and trying to cover adequately the dead who had been most inadequately covered by those who had been there before us.

The trenches had been built originally by the French and had obviously seen a lot of hard fighting at one time, they had been allowed to deteriorate into little more than drains thick with mud and rubbish and sewerage. The mud made it almost impossible to move as when it dried on your boots it became hard and heavy like cement.

It would be pointless to say that I wasn't frightened. Night and day the palms of my hands were sticky with sweat. It oozed constantly from the roots of my hair and lay in cold streaks on my forehead and neck. It wasn't the thought of my death that made me sweat, there were moments in fact that to die would have been preferable than to continue to live. I was afraid that one day I might wake up and find that I had come to accept the grotesque obscenity of the way we lived. Bennett and I shared a dug-out. It was about six feet high and eight feet long. We slept in our flea bags on a pile of comparatively dry straw that rustled all night long as if armies of creatures were marching and counter-marching through it. Bennett had an enviable facility for sleeping at any time of the night or day. He would lie there on the rustling straw, eyes shut, mouth slightly open, looking like a tired, untroubled child. I lay down because I knew I could no longer stay on my feet. I knew I had a duty to rest, but I found great difficulty in sleeping, and when I did get to sleep I would be awakened what always seemed like a few moments later by nightmares. I sound sorry for myself. I was. I worked out a system for getting through each day which consisted in concentrating on my own petty discomforts and indispositions to the exclusion of everything else except the bare bones of duty. It was the art of not looking beyond the end of your nose, and, for what it was worth, it kept me going. I have always been prone to chilblains and at this stage had them burning away not only on my fingers and toes, but also up the backs of both legs where they had been rubbed raw by my boots. I allowed the pain to obsess me completely in the hope that this way I might become blind to everything else.

Endless cups of tea laced with rum kept the cold out and the mind pretty numb. Bennett suggested one night that I should massage the backs of my legs with rum.

'The cure-all. Disinfectant, anaesthetic. I bet it would be more effective than that damn silly stuff the M.O. gave you.'

'You joke, I presume?'

'No jokes these days. No . . .'

'I think I prefer to take the cure-all internally.'

Bennett yawned.

'It's like living with a dormouse.'

He laughed.

'Why ever not? Done your rounds yet?'

'Fifteen minutes. It's a rough night for someone. There are great fireworks going on.'

He lay with his hands clasped behind his head on top of his own flea bag with mine thrown for warmth over his feet.

'Tea?' I asked him.

'I suppose so. I am rapidly becoming a tea addict. I think it will be my twelfth mug today. It's so revolting.'

I put my head out of the door. Our orderly was crouched against a low wall of sandbags, his face turned up towards the sky. For a moment it became a vicious green, flickered and then went black again.

'Tea perhaps.'

We both blinked at each other, almost blinded by the rapid change of light.

'Yes, sir.'

'Any hope of getting it without sugar?'

'I'll do my best for you, sir, but I wouldn't be too hopeful if I was you.'

'Do what you can.'

I went back in and sat down on the straw beside Bennett. His eyes were shut. The ground was never still under us and from time to time a trickle of black earth fell from the corner of the roof.

'Maybe we'll make a move soon. Maybe that's what all the banging's in aid of. Softening up the enemy. Or maybe they're softening us up. That's a rare thought.'

'Move?' His eyes remained shut. He sounded on the very edge of sleep.

'Attack. Something anyway.'

He half-laughed.

'I love you, Alec. I love the simple way in which your mind works. Oh truly, I do.'

'I'm glad I amuse you.'

'Here we've been in the trenches eight days and you say maybe we'll attack, or maybe we'll be attacked. Leave it eight months, old man.' He paused. He opened his eyes and looked at me. 'Eight years.' He sat up suddenly, creating as he did an alarming disturbance up at the back of the straw. 'We could sit here forever if they wanted us to. The fat men at home. We will attack or be attacked when they and their friends in Berlin think it expedient. The war will end when they want it to end. Or it could go on forever if that was what suited them best.'

'You exaggerate, Bennett. You've been having bad dreams.'

'Performing dogs. We're neither more nor less. A slight crack of the whip. Someone mentions the magic word, La Patrie, la Gloire, das Vaterland, Britons never shall be slaves, and the performing dogs all rush out and kill each other . . .'

'So what about becoming a hero? It doesn't leave much room for that.'

'I have come to the grim conclusion in the last few days that I will probably die ignominiously of galloping foot rot. A slow and squalid death.'

O'Keefe came in with our mugs of tea.

'There wasn't a thing I could do about the sugar, sir.'

'Can't be helped, O'Keefe.'

'It's the system,' said Bennett.

'That's right, sir. The sugar's put in with the tea, sir, all

86

mixed up like.'

'All performing dogs must have sugar in their tea.'

'Right you be, sir. It doesn't worry me, I've always been one for the sugar. Will you be doing the rounds, sir?'

'Yes.'

'You want to watch out for the rats. They say they're wild bad the night. There's been a lot of flooding up the line and they've all come, swimming in this direction.'

'Excellent,' said Bennett. 'The fellow in the straw with us here was getting a little lonely.'

'I won't need you, O'Keefe. Get some sleep if you can.'

'Very good, sir.'

He saluted and left.

'Oh my God, this tea is revolting.'

I took the rum from my pocket and passed it to him.

'The cure-all.'

'Sometimes you have sense, there's no denying it.'

He splashed the rum into his mug. His nostrils twitched with pleasure as the steam acquired the comforting smell of rum. He handed the flask back to me. I shook it, and then put it back in my pocket.

'Not having any yourself? Whyso?'

'I thought I'd save it for Jerry. It's damn cold out there.'

'Mmm. It's an odd thing, you know, Alec.'

'What's that?'

The tea was indeed revolting, sweet and stewed. It left a cloying trail down the back of my throat. I thought moment-arily of china tea in thin cups, a ring of lemon floating on the pale liquid. The smell of elegance, of security. Fingers pale and brittle as the porcelain.

'The men like you. They couldn't not like you, you're fair and decent and kind to them. You all come from different corners of the same bog, but they wouldn't follow you. Into the valley of death and all that. They don't like me, not that I care, and they won't follow me either. The only one who'll really make them forget themselves and run in the right direction when the moment comes is Glendinning. You see the dogs trust the whip crackers. I think that I shall learn to be one of them.'

He lay back in the straw again and closed his eyes.

'You do say such idiotic things.'

I wondered if he were going to fall asleep. One hand held the steaming mug pressed against his chest, the other lay quite relaxed by his side.

'What do you see when you close your eyes?'

'Dots. Millions of little dots, like coloured stars.'

'You are literal. You are truthful. You are an ass. I see the slaves rising and turning on their masters, and then do you know what?'

'What?'

I wondered if I could take my flea bag off his feet. The dampness of the straw had penetrated through to my behind which was beginning to feel cold and rather unpleasant.

'There will be singing and dancing in the streets. A sense for a time of great achievement, a flowering of all the beautiful attributes, a reaching for perfection and then baff.'

He leant his head forward slightly and took a precarious drink.

'Very obscure you are. When my eyes are shut, I see dots.'

'Baff.'

I reached over and pulled my bag off him. His feet were crusted with mud and very bony.

'Baff. The clever performing dogs pick up the whips and teach a whole new range of tricks to the rest and the whole performance starts again. C'est la bloody vie. Humorous really.'

'I don't know why you bother to go on living.'

'I think it would be realistic to say that I have anything between two minutes to six weeks. Why waste a bullet that might be put to better use? If you're not going to put that thing under your bum put it back over my feet, there's a good chap.'

I laughed and tucked it round his feet.

'They stink.'

'Never mind, when we get back to West Outre I'll wash them. Change the creeping socks.'

'Wash the creeping socks, too.'

'I think not. I haven't much love left in me for this pair.'

'You could roll them up and shoot them at the Hun. New secret weapon.'

'I will suggest it to the Major. Another drop of rum perhaps?'

'No.'

'Ttttt.'

He lifted the cup to his lips and drank again. He was the only person I have ever met who could drink lying down. He managed it most neatly. It was impossible to know what he was thinking about. Even when he was talking or rambling his face was like a clean sheet of paper, you could guess at nothing.

I finished my tea and put on my greatcoat and cap. He never opened an eye or said another word, he was too busy dancing in the streets with the risen slaves. I went out to do my rounds.

The bombardment had let up a little. The men had nothing to report. Jerry was on his own down at the furthest end of one of the trenches. The duckboarding had rotted away out there and he stood in about a foot and a half of water.

'Everything all right?'

'Yer. Thanks be to God all that shelling's over, for the moment anyway. I thought I'd never hear again.'

I handed him the flask.

'Thanks. You're a pal.'

He took a drink and handed the flask back to me.

'Finish it. It's all for you.'

He nodded. He held the flask in his hand, saving the rum till the last possible moment.

'Do you mind the swans? On the lake. You know.'

'Of course I do. What made you think of them?'

'Two came over. Just as the shelling was dying down. I heard the cracking noise of their wings.' The hand with the

89

flask drew a trail in the air, tapering off towards Ypres. 'That way they went. Low the pair of them. Just about fifteen feet up. They were swans all right.'

'You're seeing things tonight, like Bennett. Both going a bit you know.'

He took a quick drink.

'God, that's great. I have all my faculties intact, and I know a swan when I see one. Crack, crack, crack, like sheets flapping in the wind.'

Over to the right something burst into flames and a shower of sparks and light was thrown up towards the clouds.

'Hammered,' he said. 'They're really being hammered tonight. Oh Jay. I hope the mam is keeping the prayers up.'

I laughed.

'The makers of holy candles must be making a packet. Their pockets heavy with it.'

'It's nice to think that someone is benefiting.'

He spat, too close to me for my amusement.

'Damn your bloody peasant habits.'

'And damn your bloody landlord manners. Here,' he pushed the flask into my hand, 'we'll share the dregs'.

There wasn't much left to share, a mere mouth-warmer.

'How's your man Bennett?'

'I left him asleep dreaming about world revolution.'

'We'd better keep in with him. He's cute enough, that one, to be on the winning side in the end. Put that in your pocket quick, there's someone coming.'

He rubbed at his mouth with the back of his hand and turned away from me. I disposed of the flask.

'Good night, sir.' I rubbed at my mouth too, and saluted more or less simultaneously.

'Everything all right, Mr. Moore?' It was Major Glendinning.

'Yes, sir. I was just on my way back to report.'

'Barry here said it was some time since you came down this way. He thought you might have run into some trouble.'

'No trouble, sir.'

Sergeant Barry had no liking for junior officers.

'Who's that soldier there? Who is it, Barry?'

'Crowe, sir.'

'That's right,' I stupidly repeated, 'Private Crowe.'

'Ah.'

There was a long pause.

'Everything all right, Crowe?'

'Lovely, sir.'

Barry made a little whistling noise between his teeth.

'Sergeant, see that this area is duckboarded as soon as possible. Otherwise this stretch will become unusable. It's a disgrace it's been allowed to deteriorate like this.'

'It's a question of the parapet, sir . . .'

'Bloody nonsense. Let the men keep their heads down if they don't want to have them blown off. At the moment if there was an attack none of the men would be able to move here. The men must be able to move. That's important, sergeant. What good is a soldier immobilised by mud?'

'I'll see to it, sir.'

'Everything all right then, Crowe? Good fellow. Keep alert. A word with you please, Mr. Moore.'

I followed him back along the trench to his dug-out. He had a table and a chair, and his straw seemed to be slightly drier than ours. He took off his gloves and laid them neatly on the table beside a pile of papers. Like most of the officers he wore no sword, but carried a cane with him constantly which he was very quick to use if any trouble arose with the men. He threw it down now, with his cap, on to the straw. He began to unfasten the buttons of his coat. His fingers seemed to be stiff either with cold or arthritis, and he struggled with the buttons. He did not take his coat off but, as he sat down, he pulled it closer round his legs for warmth. Finally he looked at me.

'Yes,' he said.

I waited. I hoped that he wouldn't keep me for too long. The giant of tiredness was on my shoulders.

'Yes,' he repeated. His hands were locked together in front

of him. 'What's that fellow to you?'

'Sir?'

'That whatsisname? Crowe? Barry reports to me that you talk to him.'

'Well . . . yes, sir . . . I suppose I do . . .'

'What is he to you?'

There was a pause between each word that made the question very ominous.

'We come from the same village. I've known . . .'

'Let it be understood once and for all that I will have no talking between the men and the officers. Talking. You know what I mean?'

'Well . . .'

'Make it your business to understand. Discipline must be maintained. Strict impersonal discipline. At all times. In my company I will have it no other way.'

He paused and stared at me, his eyes becoming thin angry slits in his grey face.

'You are all amateurs. I will make you professionals. For me you must be one thing only. Soldiers. Nothing else matters. I will give no quarter. Understand?'

I nodded. My voice was hard to find.

'I never asked for a bunch of damn bog Irish. I must make the best of it. The men must learn. You will learn, won't you?'

'Yes, sir.'

He unclasped his hands and laid them flat, palms on the table. For a moment he studied his wrinkled fingers.

'That goes for your friend Bennett, too. You can tell him so. I will stand no tomfoolery. There was something about horses. You know what I mean . . . ?'

'Well . . .'

'I didn't listen. The man was a fool. But let there be no next time. No more tales to be told. If you give me the chance I will make soldiers out of you. Men. If you play the fool, you will see . . . as I said before, I give no quarter.'

His hand reached out towards the papers. I didn't like him,

but I saw his point. I stood rigidly to attention, fingers pointing to the floor.

'Get out,' he said.

I saluted. As I moved towards the door he spoke once more. 'Stand to arms at six thirty. We should be relieved by ten, and I don't want the company coming in here to have to spend the next ten days in our filth. Understood?'

'Understood, sir.'

Five days or so later I was lying on my mattress in West Outre. I was warm and I could smell bacon frying. There were only intermittent shells firing, somewhere quite far away. Rain thudded on the roof, but it was almost pleasant. The important thing was that someone was frying bacon, sometime soon we would eat it and drink great mugs of sweet tea. It had become imperative never to look beyond the immediate present, beyond, in fact, the bacon.

'Horses today,' said Bennett.

He was like that, one moment asleep, comfortable snores erupting from his throat, and the next wide awake and somehow well on into the day.

'Bacon,' he then said, with immense satisfaction.

It was still too dark to see him but I could hear each movement he made on his mattress as if it were amplified in some way.

'Damn you and your horses.'

'Whyso?'

'You know perfectly well whyso.'

'I feel the need to ride. My knees positively itch. I refuse to be terrorised by that . . . that . . . oh that . . . for God's sake, look at all the others who go galloping.'

'He categorically said . . .'

'It's all arranged anyway. Jerry's game, so a fig for your objections.'

I got up and lit the lamp and started on my daily examination of the chilblains. The M.O. had given me a fine white powder with which to dust them, in an effort to dry up the running sores. There had been quite an improvement in the few days we had been out of the trenches, but they were far from cured, and drove me almost mad with their itching.

'Just because you have it all arranged doesn't mean I have to come.' I began to unwind the first bandage. He didn't answer. I rolled the bandage neatly round two of my fingers as I unwound it. It was stuck in places to my leg and I had to pull quite hard to get it off, which opened up the healing sores. I wanted to cry like a child because of the fact that I was having to inflict these jabs of pain on myself.

'I will though.'

'Yes.' He didn't sound surprised.

'If you think we can get away with it.'

'But of course.'

He scrambled out of his flea bag fully clothed apart from his boots and jacket.

'Water. Ho. Water,' he shouted. He clasped both his hands in front of him and cracked each finger joint in turn. It made me feel ill. Footsteps started up the stairs.

'I find it hard to break the rules.'

I put the bandage down on the mattress beside me and looked in my kitbag for the tin of powder.

'Rules,' he repeated with contempt.

I shook the blue tin and powder floated down on to my leg. From the top of the calf to the ankle pus and blood glistened in the light.

'I should cut it off,' advised Bennett kindly. 'Then they might send you home.'

'Oh, shut up.'

The door opened and O'Keefe came in with a steaming jug of water.

'Morning, sirs, one and all.'

'Good morning. In the basin, there's a good chap. Not very generous, are you? Leave a drop in the jug for the teeth. I feel like polishing up the old choppers today.'

'Right you be, sir.'

The soldier poured the water carefully into a small metal bowl, put the jug down beside it on the table, saluted and left. Bennett went over and looked at the water without any pleasure. 'Just like being back at school. At least the water's warm here. None of the cold splash splash, windows open, smile it's good for you out here. That's where you missed out you know, old man. At school one learns a healthy disrespect for authority. Not much else. Your head is stuffed with book learning for what it's worth. Cricket. Now there's a civilised game.'

'We don't really play cricket at home.'

'Of course not. I said it was a civilised game. Let me tell you, the better you are at cricket the farther you'll go.'

'I don't want to go very far.'

'That is something you never know until you start going.'

He lathered soap over his face and what was visible of his neck, then he rubbed and pummelled at himself with his strong thin finger.

'I shall be clean. I shall. I shall.' It was like an incantation. He bent and stared at his clown's face in the spotted mirror that O'Keefe had attached to the wall for us. His eyes were bloodshot. My eyes were bloodshot. Everyone's eyes for miles around were bloodshot. I considered whether to replace the old bandage which was rather unpleasant to look at or use one of my precious clean ones. I decided to postpone the decision until after I had eaten.

'Damn bleeding gums. It's always been the same. We used to stand in a row at school. Scrub, scrub, spit. Hardly a chap didn't have bleeding gums. Odd really. Another thing you've missed finding out about your fellow men.'

'I reckon I'll learn it all from you. If you're spared, I'll learn.'

'A teacher of anarchy to a gentle conservative. What a role.'

I blushed.

'I'm not a Tory, you idiot. I'm a Home Ruler.'

He yelled with laughter.

'And what the hell is that?'

'You know as well as I do.'

'A sort of ineffectual political splinter group.'

'Parnell...'

'... is dead, and anyway...' He stopped talking and blotted at his face with a grey exhausted towel, then he turned round towards me. 'Anyway he was useless. He let himself be killed. What sort of a man is that?'

He threw the towel down on the floor and came over to me. He put his hand lightly on my head. A cross between a benediction and a caress.

'I never expected to admire gentleness in a man.' He let his hand fall to his side. 'Don't misunderstand me in any way.' The lamp began to smoke, automatically I stretched out my hand and adjusted the flame. He stood quite still beside me. On the little finger of his left hand he wore a gold signet ring. It looked almost too heavy for his fragile bones. 'Don't misjudge.' He moved abruptly away from me. Just a step. There was a slight smile on his face. I said nothing, only because I didn't know what to say, and it seemed like a moment when the right thing had to be said ... or nothing.

He groped in his pocket and pulled out his comb and then went back across the room to the mirror. He had to bend slightly at the knees to get his face in the glass.

'Probably such things would normally be left unsaid. But these are not normal circumstances. Don't feel you have to react in any way. I think I will definitely grow a moustache.'

I was left with the confusion in my mind that perhaps he had thought more than he had said, that perhaps he was trying to undermine me in some way, that perhaps he was merely making a simple spontaneous statement of affection to which I was unable to react. In the life that I had always known, spontaneity and warmth were unknown, almost anarchic, qualities. Dangerous. I powdered my left leg carefully.

'Don't you think it would suit me?'

'Ah ... oh ... yes.'

'Drooping Victorian variety.'

'Splendid.'

'I have annoyed you.'

'No.'

'What a pity.'

I decided to replace the old dirty bandages after all.

'So you'll ride with us.'

'Yes. I said yes.'

'So you did. Where the hell's that bacon? The smell is driving me mad.'

I met them at the same corner as before. This time, though, Bennett had taken Jerry with him. There were heavy green snow clouds. The air was still and bitingly cold. I had brought a pair of gloves for Jerry which I handed to him before I mounted.

'I'm going to try and get transferred to the horse lines.'

'Hark at him,' said Bennett.

'They're not looking after those animals at all. My God, Alec, you ought to see the place. It's a disgrace. You can tell by just looking at these three. The spirit's gone out of them.'

'They had a hit . . .'

'Fifteen killed and another twenty or more had to be shot.'

'Irish sentiment creeping in.'

'Laugh your head off if you want to.'

'Sorry, old chap. No offence meant.'

'The smell would sicken you. Even now I feel as if I had it all around me.'

'Dead horses don't smell any worse than dead men.'

'Ah shut up, can't you.'

'Leave him alone, Bennett.'

'Perspective is needed. You damn Celts have none. It's no wonder we don't think you're fit to rule yourselves.'

'We all came to enjoy ourselves. It's not even raining. Let's just get on and do it.'

'Righty ho.'

Bennett dug his heels into his horse, turned right over a small drain and was away off across a wide field. The horses laboured in the mud but once we got on to the slightly higher ground they went well. They seemed to become revitalised. Jerry, crouching low, edged past me and was soon up beside Bennett. My legs were hurting with the sudden new pressures on them so I slowed down to a canter and watched the other two making for a ditch which they cleared in a spray of mud. At the best of times that winter countryside would have been uninspiring, but at that moment it seemed like the acres that must lie before the doors of hell, or indeed heaven, the place we wander until we forget the earth. I hoped I wouldn't have to spend too much time there. I had lost touch with the horse beneath me and he had slowed his canter to a trot. The other two had disappeared. Two small flakes of snow whirled towards me and landed on my greatcoat. I watched them die and then pulled myself together. The horse responded. He seemed to know which way his companions had gone and I let him take me to them.

'What happened to you?' asked Bennett.

'I was just taking my own time.'

'He beat me.'

'Yes, and will again.'

'We'll see.'

'There's a village beyond looks as if it might have a bar,' suggested Jerry.

'A worthy thought,' said Bennett.

The village lay along the edge of the fields, apparently untouched by the war. High walls hid barns and farmyards from the road. Stern windows glittered as we passed, glass intact, shutters peeling with neglect. Black-clothed women moved cautiously behind the glass, peered to see the horsemen in their private street. Jerry was right, there was, of course, a bar. We tied up the horses and went in. It was dark but warm. Behind a zinc-topped bar with a brass rail a man stood forlornly wiping at some glasses. He gave us a brief smile, polite, but hardly friendly.

'Messieurs.'

Three old men were playing cards in the corner, their voices low, a bottle between them for which they reached in turn.

'I suppose brandy's the thing to set us up.' Bennett went over to the bar. Jerry and I sat down and opened our coats.

'Une bouteille de cognac, s'il vous plaît.'

The glass wiper came out with a rush of words which Bennett was obviously unable to follow. The man shrugged and disappeared into the back of the bar. Bennett came over and sat down beside us.

'Odd damn place. Where's the war? What's happened to the war?'

A faint smell of Eau de Javel drifted up from the floor. A woman shouted something in the back of the house. A villainous-looking dog padded in from the street. It crossed the floor and collapsed against the bar, worn out by living. Like most of the other dogs we saw around it looked as if it could do with a square meal.

The proprietor materialised out of the darkness, bottle in hand. He put it on our table and stood looking at us.

'Merci . . . ah, merci . . .' I could feel Mr. Bingham's disapproval fussing around me.

'. . . beaucoup.'

'Où est la guerre?' asked Bennett.

Carefully the man pulled a large white handkerchief out of his pocket. He examined it for a moment before blowing his somewhat unattractive nose. When he had finished he folded the handkerchief neatly and returned it to his pocket.

'Vous rigolez, monsieur,' he suggested.

'What the hell is he on about?' muttered Jerry in my direction. 'And where's the glasses? Cut the cackle and ask for glasses.'

Bennett ignored this practical suggestion.

'Non. Je ne rigole pas. Où est la guerre. Où?'

'La guerre est partout, monsieur.' He spread his arms wide, embraced the room, the village, his whole world sadly between them. I reached out for the bottle and pulled the cork. The warm smell of brandy enriched the air between us.

'Glasses,' said Jerry hopefully. No one reacted.

'Où est la guerre?'

Jerry picked up an imaginary glass from the table and took a quick drink from it. The Frenchman nodded.

'Bien sûr.' He went behind the bar and rattled around for a moment. As he passed the dog it thumped its bedraggled tail once on the floor.

'Tooralooraloo, tooralooralay, tooralooraloo, tooralooralay,' sang Jerry with sudden gaiety.

The card players turned and looked at him with surprise.

'And the song he sang was The Jug of Punch.'

The owner came back with three glasses which he placed in a straight line on the table. He picked up the bottle and carefully filled each glass to the brim.

'Voilà.'

'La guerre n'est pas ici.'

My hand and Jerry's stretched out simultaneously for our glasses. Mine, as usual, shook slightly. His was steady as a rock.

'Mais pourquoi? Why?'

'Nous attendons, monsieur. Jour par jour, nous attendons. Les Boches, les Belges, les Anglais, même les Français, qui que ce soit, tout le monde souffrira ici.'

'Sláinte.'

'Mud in your eye.'

'Nous avons perdu notre fils. Le vingt septembre.'

'Je regrette . . .'

'N'en parlons plus. C'est fini.'

'How about a drink for the old fella?'

'His son was killed,' I said.

Jerry crossed himself.

'God rest his soul.'

The man smiled at him. For the first time a real smile.

I pushed Bennett's drink towards him.

'Pour vous, monsieur.'

He picked it up without a word and threw the liquid into his mouth without apparently touching the glass with his lips. He put the glass back on the exact spot he had picked it up from. It was all over in a flash.

'On a besoin.'

He pulled the handkerchief out again and wiped his mouth. He bowed towards us with solemnity and retired behind the bar. The dog once more moved its tail as his master passed. I poured out a glass for Bennett.

'Thanks.'

He looked at it seriously for a moment before picking it up, almost as if he were considering whether to touch it or not.

'Tooralooraloo, tooralooralay . . .'

'Are you also a Home Ruler?'

'Me? Jay?' Jerry spat on the floor and began to laugh. Bennett grinned and swallowed his brandy at one gulp. He filled his glass again.

'What gave you that idea?'

'Alexander here.'

'Ah sure, God love him. He doesn't know if he's coming or going. He's been brought up to trust the British. The honourable people.'

'Well, your father's in the army, isn't he? He must feel much the same.'

'My father never had a chance to find, let alone use, his five wits. Pass over the bottle.'

'If you're not a Home Ruler, what are you?'

'A Republican.'

I pushed the bottle over to him. Bennett looked surprised.

'Are there many of them?'

'A good few.'

'Be honest, Jerry, a handful.'

'You know nothing about it, Alec.'

'I read the papers.'

'The papers.'

Bennett leaned across the table towards him.

'I don't honestly see what you're doing here then.'

'Learning to shoot a gun. Lookit.' He took a drink before speaking again. 'When I go back I'll be one of the fellas really knows what the hell he's doing when it comes to fighting. It's all very well marching around in the hills with hurling sticks, but the moment's going to come when it'll be handy to have some men around who can do more than that. Maybe they'll make me a general.' He started to laugh. 'By Jesus, I'll tell you one thing, if I come out of this alive I'll never be frightened again.'

'Bang goes our stud farm,' I heard myself say mournfully.

'That'll be all right.' He put out his hand and touched mine. 'There'll be time enough for what we want to do when we've done what we have to do.'

'I am delightfully amazed,' said Bennett.

'Did you ever hear tell of Patrick Pearse?'

'I can't say I did.'

'He's a great hand at putting things in an electrifying sort of way. He's a schoolmaster. Now he said, not too long ago . . .' he picked thoughtfully at his nose while he collected the words '. . . there are things more horrible than bloodshed, and slavery is one of them. They stick in your mind, words like that.'

'But slavery . . . honestly, Jerry . . . who is a slave . . . ?' I stopped and looked at them both. Bennett was doing some glass filling. 'According to Bennett here, we're all slaves because we're too frightened to be free men.'

'I'm not talking about philosophy but about actuality.'

'Nonsense, there are no slaves in Ireland.'

'We haven't the right to speak for ourselves. What's that only a form of slavery?'

'Home Rule . . .'

'I shit on your Home Rule. If it ever happens it will only be a sop. Keep them quiet. I believe . . . I know the only way to get them out is to shoot them out.'

'Isn't it odd that all the time we've been friends we've never had this conversation before.'

'Perhaps it's as well. It'll do neither of us any harm now

and it might have before.'

'I can't believe there are many think as you do.'

'There will be. Maybe even yourself.'

'Who knows?'

'Well, I must say I'm charmed and delighted to meet a fellow revolutionary,' said Bennett. 'Shake,' he held his hand across the table to Jerry, who merely looked at it and smiled. 'I like the sound of your Mr. Whatsit.'

'Pearse.'

'Perhaps if I don't succeed in becoming a hero in Flanders I'll come and be one in Ireland.'

Jerry laughed.

'I'd say we'll have a few of them. On whose side, may I ask?'

'Mr. Pearse's side, of course. The side of the man who said those words.'

'I don't believe he said them for reasons you'd understand.'

'Fiddlesticks.'

'You're both mad.'

'Let's drink to our folly.'

Bennett picked up the bottle and waved it towards the man behind the bar.

'Monsieur?'

'Merci.' He shook his head.

'Sláinte,' said Jerry again.

'To each one's dream,' said Bennett.

'People will sneer perhaps at the shortness of their necks, but they'll win. All over the world.'

'What's that?' asked Bennett surprised.

'My horses. I don't have your sort of dream. Just my lovely unbeatable horses.'

'We'll do it yet so we will, and I'll ride them whether you like my style or not, Mr. Bennett.'

'Ascot, Epsom, Newmarket, Cheltenham, Longchamps . . . Saratoga even. How about Saratoga, Jerry?'

'Right you be.'

'You're probably drunk,' said Bennett.

'Probably.'

'Here's to your horses. Winners all.'

'Sláinte.'

'I hope the beasts we have today know their way home.'

'My little grey home in the west,' sang Jerry.

'Sssh, you're frightening the card players.'

'Da dee da da dee da da . . .'

'Je vous en prie . . .'

'It's all right, monsieur,' said Bennett. 'Ne vous inquiétez pas. He is a little drunk and a little malheureux. Il est Irlandais, you understand, and the Irlandais chantent toujours quand ils sont un peu drunk.'

The owner stood, only his hand moved, eternally polishing glasses that couldn't possibly be dirty. Maybe he was listening, maybe he wasn't. Maybe he was thinking of his son killed on the twentieth of September, when I was training my Morrigan on the hills at home, and Jerry was going on manoeuvres with a hurling stick. Jerry hummed just below his breath. The card players looked uneasily towards us from time to time. I got the feeling they looked upon us as some advance party of the unwanted war. They wished we would go. Their wish filled the bar and made me uneasy. A rattle of hail, like musketry fire on the windows, made Jerry shiver. He reached for the bottle and filled our glasses once more.

'One for the road. Sláinte.'

'To the dead.' Bennett raised his glass.

'How ghoulish. It's the living need your thoughts.'

'To the living dead then.'

The three men in the corner turned once more and watched us as we drank the toast. Their eyes were like the windows of French houses, secretive. Bennett shoved the cork into the brandy bottle and rose. He put the bottle in the pocket of his greatcoat. He went over to the bar and put some money down in front of the proprietor.

'Eh bien,' he said. 'Nous allons chercher la guerre. Nous allons massacrer les sales Boches. Peut-être nous reviendrons.'

'Peut-être,' repeated the man behind the bar without much

enthusiasm. The dog growled softly to itself. Having lost the war I never wanted to find it again, but we slipped back into it as easily as we had slipped out of it.

The next morning we stood to in the breaking dawn. An east wind carrying hail made the men restless. Major Glendinning with Barry at his shoulder spoke a few words.

'A sorry lot.'

There was a very long pause. Some poor bastard tried to stifle a cough, and it was as much as I could do to prevent my fingers tearing at the backs of my legs.

'Canaille, I think our allies the French would say. The . . . ah . . . onus is on us to show the world that appearances aren't everything. Yes, Sergeant Barry?'

'Yes, sir.'

Barry glared round, obviously hoping to find some dissenter in the ranks.

'Believe me, I understand your exasperation . . . your impatience. The apparent futility of inactivity has to be borne, and you will bear it, and when it comes to fighting, which it will do, you will fight. Anyone who thinks otherwise will have me to reckon with, and I warn you all, here and now, that I have no scruples about meting out the ultimate. Understand. No scruples whatsoever. Ultimate.' He enjoyed using that word. I hoped that the men realised, as I did, that he was not a man to throw idle threats around. 'We leave for the front at ten. Mr. Bennett and Mr. Moore will make sure that no packs are jettisoned for any reason.' The fools tended, if the going got too hard, to drop what they considered to be the least important articles in their load in the nearest ditch.

A cock crew. An absurdly normal sound. The clouds were low and moving fast over our heads. As the darkness melted I could see that they were still green and snow-filled.

The Major tapped his cane against his boot.

'Now,' he said, almost as if he meant it, 'if anyone has any questions . . .' He left the words hanging on the air with the steam that burst from between his lips as he spoke.

Jerry stepped forward a pace and saluted.

'Who's this? What's this?'

Barry leaned towards him and muttered in his ear.

'Private Crowe, sir. You know.'

'Quite. Ah . . . yes. Crowe.' He stared at Jerry as if he were seeing him for the first time. 'Speak up, man.'

'I wondered, sir, would it be possible like, to transfer into the horse lines?'

I blushed.

'Am I to take it, man, that you are in some way dissatisfied with . . .' He gestured abruptly with one hand. The men's faces were expressionless.

'It's not that, sir. I only feel I could be better occupied there. I seen the horse lines, sir. They're in a bad way. I could help out. Horses . . .' His voice faded. They both stared at each other.

'They need someone like me there,' he said finally. His voice was very firm, very contained.

'Might I ask what you were doing in the horse lines?'

'I just went there, sir. It's like I said, I have an interest . . .'

'In finding an easy billet?'

'I beg your pardon, sir, nothing was further from my mind.'

'In that case, Crowe, or whatever your damn name is, you won't mind staying where you are.'

Jerry didn't speak, merely nodded slightly.

'What was that you said? Speak up, man.'

'I said nothing, sir.'

'I've had my eye on you for some time as a potential trouble-maker. Well, I warn you. Yes.'

He seemed to have finished. The cougher tried once more to smother his cough. Sergeant Barry bit fiercely at the corner of his moustache.

'Yes.' He turned to Barry. 'Keep an eye on this soldier.'

'Yes, sir.'

Nothing would give him more pleasure.

106

'See the men are ready to leave at ten, Mr. Bennett.'

'Sir.'

The Major turned and walked away, the cane twitching in his hand as if it had a life of its own.

Bennett fell the men out and we went for breakfast.

'God, Jerry's a fool.'

There were sausages and fried corned beef and potatoes for breakfast. The condemned men's belly full. I had received a letter from my mother which I was endeavouring to read. She always writes with the thinnest of nibs and the words have the look of live insects grappling with each other all over the white pages rather than decipherable words. The paper was thick and square and was faintly scented, a smell from her hands rather than anything more obvious and possibly vulgar. The corned beef was vile.

'Ummm.'

'You're not listening.'

'The corned beef is vile. They might have found us an egg or two for our last meal.'

Bennett shouted across the room to O'Keefe who was sitting with the men at another table.

'Any eggs there for Mr. Moore?'

'Eggs? What's eggs?'

'A damn fool.' Bennett lowered his voice as he turned to me. 'Hey? Don't you think so?'

'It might have worked.'

'Not for a second. He's got himself labelled now, and what's more, Barry doing heavy breathing round every corner.'

'. . . the Daly boy came home on crutches, he had a hole blown in his leg, somewhere near you I suppose. He seems remarkably gay about the whole thing. Henry Townsend is missing. You are all so brave. Several of the girls from round about have gone to join the V.A.D. Soon there will be no young people left round here at all. Maud stayed for three weeks. Nice as she is I found it a little too long . . .'

'You know the theory of the scapegoat?'

'. . . It is too long since you have written. We all long to hear whatever news you can tell us. I, in fact, feel wounded by your silence. Everyone else seems to have time to write . . .'

'Hey?'

'Shut up for God's sake, Bennett. I'm trying to read a letter from home.'

He leaned across the table, over the cooling plates of corned beef and the steaming tea. His rum bottle was by his cup I noticed. I hadn't yet got into the way of rum for breakfast but it was presumably only a matter of time. He pulled the letter from my hand.

'What is home? A rhetorical question which I will answer myself. The unreality of unrealities. The likelihood is that neither you nor I nor Jerry will ever see home again. If we do we will see it as different people. Therefore news from home is meaningless.'

'Oh, come . . .'

He tore my letter into small square pieces, a frown creasing the pale skin of his forehead as his hands moved and moved again. I just sat quietly and watched. He threw the paper scraps behind him on to the floor. Confetti. The soldiers at the other table watched with indifference. He smiled at me suddenly and reached out his destructive hand towards me.

'Why don't you hit me?'

'I don't know.'

For a moment he looked as if he were going to tell me, and then thought better of it. He picked up his cup instead and drained it down his throat. Then he got up.

'Look sharp,' he said across his shoulder to the men as he left the room.

I listened to his boots on the stone stairs. They struck sparks in my head as he climbed. The table at which we ate, drank, wrote, sprawled, waiting, was pale and furrowed with age and the scrubbing brushes of several generations of prideful women. The patterns of the wood and wearing lay gracefully on it, almost like the work of some artist. We had stained it with our mugs and glasses, brown rings and grey and, at one end, a cluster of cigarette burns. One damn fool had cut his initials deep into it with a knife. K.D., wounding, with three heavy lines scored below. Someone had spilled a blot of ink and then turned the blue stain into a crawling creature. We hadn't long left. Bennett's feet above my head were urgent. I pulled a piece of paper from my pocket, and my pen, and began to write to my mother. I wrote a detailed description of the table at which I sat. At that moment it seemed very important.

The snow started to come down in gusts about nine forty-five. It made the going pretty tough. We didn't get to the support trenches until after dark. The men were whacked and hungry. Hard little fringes of snow clung to their hair, their collars, the edges of their greatcoats . . . The chaps we were replacing were in a hurry to get away and the briefing was curt. They had had a bad time. Three men lost and seven wounded. They only wanted to get out, away, back to the comparative safety of the farm. They resented the fact we had made them wait even a minute longer than they had to.

It was my bad luck to be detailed up to the front. We went without even a cup of tea. The trenches were in a mess. There had obviously been some hard shelling. It would take a couple of days' work to get the parapets rebuilt and the lines cleared of debris. Out beyond the wire a man was screaming. Not a prolonged scream, it rose and fell, faded, deteriorated into a babbling from time to time and then occasionally there was silence. During the silence you could never forget the scream, only wait for it to start again. The men hated the sound as much as I. You could see the hate on their faces.

I had finished my rounds and was about to try and get a couple of hours' sleep when Jerry appeared in the doorway. He had a mug of tea in his hand, which he handed to me. His hands were shaking.

'What's up?'

'I must be getting old.'

'Sit down.'

I pointed at the pile of straw.

'May I?'

'Damn you, Jerry, sit down.'

We sat down side by side. The tea steamed calmly between us.

'Legs bad?'

'They could be worse.'

'That bugger yelling gets on your nerves.'

'I'm sorry about this morning, Jerry. I should have said something. I know I should.'

'That would have made two eejits instead of one. You did better to keep your mouth shut.'

'Have a drink.'

'I wouldn't say no.'

I got up and opened my kit bag. The rum was wrapped in an old green jersey. I put the bottle down on the floor and threw the jersey to Jerry.

'For me?'

'No point in being colder than you have to.'

'Shove some of that in my tea. You'll have to use the flask.'

'I tried to get a line on him, but in the dark it's impossible.'

He unscrewed the lid and poured a good measure into my mug. It would cool the tea, but who cared.

'Who?'

'Your man beyond. I thought maybe I could put him out. But it's out of the question. They say he's been going on like that for two days. Five of them went out.'

'Oh.'

'I hoped like . . . you know . . .'

'Yes.'

'But I couldn't.'

'Maybe it's as well.'

He laughed and took a long drink from the bottle.

'None of them came back.'

We were both silent for a long time.

'It's a sod,' he said.

'Soon it'll be over. They say soon. There'll be a big push and then . . .'

'Do you remember anything? Grass that hasn't been

walked on? Calm faces? Silence?'

'The swans.'

'Yes. God, that stuff's good, I was famished with the cold. A good turf fire would be great now. Off with the boots and stretch out your legs to it.'

'We never knew when we were well off.'

'Oh Jay.'

'Have some more.'

He nodded and took a drink.

'Where's your man Bennett?'

'I suppose he's running round in rings for the old man.'

'Old bastard. I tell you, when this war is over I'll have a bullet or two for the likes of him. We'll have them running for their lives.'

'I don't know how you can contemplate ever fighting again.'

'It won't be like this. There'll be no trenches, no front lines. No waiting. Every town, every village will be the front line. Hill, rock, tree. They won't know which way to look. Even the children, for God's sake, will fight them. It won't be like this, I promise you that. Oh, Alec, it's some thought.'

'I hate your vision.'

'Hate away, man.'

'You both seem to get some obscure pleasure from violence, or the thought of it anyway.'

'Hunting?'

'A kind of mad perfection.'

'But violent, Alec.'

'I suppose I don't think things out very clearly.'

'You will.' His voice was brusque.

'Maybe it's a kind of lack of energy.'

'We just get to work differently. We need each other though. Your kind and mine. You'll see.'

'You make me uneasy. Much more uneasy than Bennett.'

'He's a bag of wind. One day he'll blow himself out.'

He stood up.

'I must get back. I'm glad the legs aren't too bad. Anything

111

I can do?'

'No thanks.'

He picked up my mug.

'I'll see you so.'

'Yes.'

He moved slowly to the door. I wanted him to stay. I didn't want to be alone. He turned at the door and smiled at me. Lifted a tired grey hand in mock salute.

'Will that be all, sir?'

'All. Yes. All.'

As he pushed aside the boards that formed the door a cold little wind came in and fidgeted round, bringing with it the sound of laughter.

'For God's sake, Jerry, tell them to shut up. Where do they think they are?'

He pulled the door quickly into place behind him.

I lay down and closed my eyes. Coloured flowers danced and twirled in the blackness. My legs burned. The screaming, I think, continued, or maybe it was inside my head.

Bennett arrived next morning, all cheerful.

'Well, here we are again. Holidays with pay.'

'Is the old man coming?'

'On his way. On his way. You've got a hell of a mess to clear up here.'

'Mmm.'

We had been working like the devil since first light. Propping the walls where they had caved in, planking over the worst of the mud, filling sandbags and dragging them what seemed like miles along the trenches. There were two snipers at work also, and we had to crouch almost double to avoid drawing their fire. Leaden rain fell continuously. Up the line, not far enough away, the big guns had started pounding as soon as it had become light enough to see a few yards.

'What's all that?'

He jerked his head towards the scream.

'They say he's been at it for four days.'

'Christ. Is he one of ours?'

I nodded.

'Oh Christ again.'

He poked at the corner of his right eye with a finger.

'Or Jay as some might say.'

'Quite.'

'There are rumours of an attack.'

'I suppose if they've reached the likes of you they've also reached the Hun.'

'Likely enough.'

'A happy prospect.'

'Ah well,' he said, 'look on the bright side, anything's better than sitting around.'

The rumours were probably correct. All day long shells flew high over our heads, obviously aimed at some target a couple of miles behind us, like a possible build-up of men or artillery. We heard the whistle of them without alarm by then. Our job was unpleasant enough to keep our minds off danger. One of the stretches of the wall that had collapsed had left raw to the world the remains of what had been a dozen or so French men. We packed them neatly away behind more sandbags and hoped that they wouldn't appear in our lives again.

Major Glendinning did not arrive with us until after dark. I stood up as he came in and saluted.

'Anything to report?'

'Not really, sir. We've spent most of the day repairing . . .'

'Quite.'

He threw his hat down on the table and unbuttoned his coat.

'Tea?'

'Yes, sir.'

I went to the door and called to O'Keefe who was hovering around outside.

'No milk, no sugar.'

113

I passed on his request, and hoped for the best. When I turned back into the dug-out he was settled on the only chair, his coat neatly draped across the back, some papers spread on the table in front of him. He took a small package out of his pocket and put it on the table. With care he unwrapped a large white handkerchief and produced a lemon. He proceeded to cut two neat rings off it with a small sharp knife. Having done this he wiped the blade of the knife carefully on a corner of the handkerchief and wrapped the lemon up and put it back in the pocket of his jacket.

'We all have our idiosyncrasies. Don't hover, boy, don't hover. Sit down.'

I began to gather up my pieces of paper from the table where they had been lying when he came in.

'What's all this?' he asked, with a certain interest in his voice.

'I just try to write a bit, sir . . . nothing very . . . just . . . you know.'

I shoved the lot into my kit-bag.

'Memos, no doubt, to Brigade Headquarters, if not the War Office, on how to run the war, by a junior officer. A very junior officer.'

I blushed.

'Oh no, sir, nothing like that at all. I just write, sir, for pleasure. Nothing you . . . well, nothing you . . .'

'Could take exception to.'

'That's right, sir.'

O'Keefe came in with two mugs of tea. He put them carefully on the table. I noticed that one of them had no milk, I was sure it had no sugar either, I was also sure that I would find I had the same old brew.

'Will that be all, sir?'

'That will be all.'

Major Glendinning speared the two rings of lemon with the point of his knife and dropped them into the mug.

'Well sit, for God's sake.'

I took my mug and sat down on the straw.

'So you've nothing to report?'

'No, sir.'

'I've had a look, Moore, it's not bad. What's been done. You'll have to press on with it tomorrow. Full speed. They're going to be sending considerably more troops up here quite soon.'

'An attack?'

'Field officers are only allowed to speculate. They receive orders, seldom information. Speculation either drives you on, or drives you mad. I shall spend the night here. Can you find me a sleeping bag?'

'I'll do my best, sir. You can have mine and I'll get one from one of the men.'

'As you please. Well, away and see what you can do. I have a report to write up, then I will turn in.'

He gave me a ferocious little smile.

I left him to his report and his lemon tea. I also left my tea, which annoyed me, as I was sure that he would regard it as somewhat lackadaisical to take it with me.

Jerry was sitting against the sandbags playing his mouth organ softly. It was a tune I knew in my bones but couldn't put a name to. The others were lolling or lying on the straw waiting for sleep. Jerry cast an eye at me but went on playing, his hands fluttering round the edge of his mouth like butterflies. Some of the men looked up, others paid no heed. I spoke to O'Keefe.

'Any hope of some bedding. The Major's going to spend the night with us. Would there be a flea bag going begging?'

'If it was only fleas in them bags how lucky we'd be,' said one of the men.

'Leave it to me, sir. I'll see that neither you nor the Major goes cold.'

Outside, the rain had stopped. The air was dank and filled with smoke. The scream rose for a moment to an almost inhuman note. Behind me one of the men swore ferociously.

'Mr. Moore.'

The Major's voice like a sharp metal probe touched a nerve

in my brain. I went in to him. He was sitting there, his head tilted slightly to one side, listening carefully.

'Who is that?'

'It's one of the Gloucesters, sir. Five of them went out on a recce. Four days ago now, sir. I really don't think he can be conscious.'

'Thank you,' he said sarcastically.

O'Keefe came in behind me with a sleeping bag and a blanket.

'Thank you,' I said. 'Put them over there by mine.'

He nodded.

'We'll go out and see to him when I've finished my report.'

'Oh.'

O'Keefe folded the blanket neatly before putting it down on the straw. He listened.

'Give me half an hour, perhaps a little less. Don't turn in.'

'But . . .'

'I can ask for a volunteer.'

'Oh no . . . I . . . but what can we do?'

He picked up his knife and tucked it into a neat leather pouch on his belt.

'We can make no decisions until we make ourselves fully aware of the situation. Now, if you'll forgive me. O'Keefe.'

'Sir.'

'Have a couple of men stand to in half an hour. Mr. Moore and I will need cover. Sensible men. Not damn stupid fools.'

'Sir.' He saluted and went out.

The Major continued to cover the pages in front of him with neat thin words. Black ink, black pen held like some surgical instrument in his neat thin fingers. I got a book out of my kitbag and tried to read. I was quite unable to concentrate. I read the words over and over with my eyes, but they never got further than that. I mouthed them almost aloud. I even tried each word with a finger but it made no difference, they remained merely disconnected words thrown in tidy lines on the page. I will never remember what it was that I was trying to read. I am afraid to see what makes him scream was all that was held in my mind. I am afraid I will remember that for ever. I am afraid to be reduced myself to that.

'That's that.' He patted all his papers into a neat pile. 'We'd better take a look at the weather. No point in sticking our necks out too far.' He stood up and stretched. He looked at me with speculation as he brought his arms down.

'Pistol?'

I nodded. I touched it, just to make sure.

'Loaded, I presume?'

He was pulling at his moustache with his fingers, stretching it also, down over his thin mouth.

'Yes, sir.'

'Torch? Splendid. Then let's get on. Waste no more time. Leave your greatcoat. Merely a hindrance on an outing of this sort. Just follow me and do exactly as I say. Exactly.'

O'Keefe was outside waiting with Jerry and another soldier. They carried their rifles at the ready. It was a perfect night for creeping in the dark. Storm clouds hid the sky and the rain was beginning to fall again. My hands were shaking. I shoved them into my pockets.

'Good. Couldn't be better. If we're not back in reasonable time . . . or if you've any reason to think . . . ah . . . O'Keefe . . .'

'Yes, sir.'

'Send word at once to Mr. Bennett. Understood?'

'Sir.'

'We'll either bring him in or . . .'

Jerry's hand closed briefly round my elbow in salutation.

'All right, Moore?'

'All right, sir.'

I followed him over the parapet. A scramble rather than a climb. I heard the two soldiers move into place behind us. I heard the click of their rifles.

'You got your torch there?' He spoke in a whisper. 'Here, man, here. Shine it low. Keep your hand shading it. There, that'll do. Off now. Lower. On. A little lower. Right you be.'

He cut the wire in several places and slipped through. I

followed, feeling the barbs tugging at my trousers and jacket. Stay here with us. Stay. Away on our right something was burning fiercely. The undercurves of the clouds were stained orange and sparks danced in the air. In front of me the Major, stooping almost double, had started to run. The ground was pitted with shell holes, but he seemed to be able to see them in the dark. The main thing was, not merely to keep from falling into the holes, but not to be squeamish about what you walked on. I tried to think of nothing but the bulk of his back moving before me through the blackness. The wounded man was no longer screaming. Long exhausted sobs were all we could hear now. It seemed to take an age to find him. Somewhere there was a burst of rifle fire, and then after a moment an answering burst, but it was far away, background chatter. If they put up a flare or two, just for the hell of it, we would be finished, sitting ducks. We found him at last on the edge of a shell hole.

'Ah,' grunted the Major suddenly. He went down on his knees. I crouched beside him, still staring at the back of his jacket.

'Torch. Hold it right down close to the ground. Here, get round to the other side. Mind the damn hole.'

I felt my way round what was left of the man on the ground. He was quite oblivious to our arrival.

'Torch. Now, man.'

As the light hit his face the man began to scream again. I caught a glimmer of a wild blue eye and a splitting mouth.

'Run it slowly down his body. I don't think there's much hope. Down. Along this way. I must be sure. Oh, Jesus Christ.'

I could see his hands moving slowly, two browsing animals. He fumbled for a moment and then shoved some sodden papers into my hand.

'Keep them. Hold the torch steady, damn you. By God, if only they'd given me soldiers instead of children.'

There was a small clink of metal on metal, infinitesimal.

'Far off most secret and inviolate Rose.'

'Shut up.'

118

I hadn't realised that I had spoken aloud. The Major groaned suddenly, or sighed rather, a long sad sigh and the screaming stopped. There was for a moment total silence except for the plash of the falling rain.

'Put the bloody thing out.'

I switched off the torch.

'Wait a moment till we adjust our focus and then follow me. Keep right down.'

We reached the wire safely and through. The three waiting men helped us over the parapet. Major Glendinning pushed past them.

'Hot water,' he growled over his shoulder. 'I don't care where you get it but get it quickly, and a cup of tea for Mr. Moore.' He laughed nastily.

Back in the dug-out the first thing he did was to produce yet another amazingly white handkerchief and proceed to clean his knife.

'Get out of those clothes or we'll have you down with pneumonia.'

Obediently I removed all my clothes and wrapped myself in my greatcoat. I lay down on top of my flea bag and watched him polishing and polishing. His face was expressionless, but white. The polishing was necessary to him. When the knife seemed clean enough he laid it on the table beside his pile of papers. He rolled the handkerchief into a ball and threw it into the corner where it lay disregarded in the straw. He began to unbutton his jacket. His fingers were barely working, stained.

'Poetry,' he said with anger.

'It was more like an incantation . . . a sort of prayer. I didn't realise . . .'

'You are a dismal creature, Moore.' The sound of that pleased him. He repeated it. 'A dismal creature . . . Yes.'

'Perhaps if we had met under other circumstances . . .'

O'Keefe came in with a bucket of water and a tin basin.

'Pour half of it out and leave it on the table. Mr. Moore can use the bucket. Can you get these clothes dry for us?'

'I'll do my best, sir.'

'Good man.'

He was all affability, charming smiles. He stripped to his underpants and O'Keefe collected up our clothes and took them away. He took off his wrist watch and laid it meticulously beside the knife. His arms were stained up almost as far as the elbow with what I presumed to be a mixture of mud and blood. He plunged them into the basin and stood quite still letting the warmth seep up into his shoulders. I knew I should get up and wash too, but I couldn't bring myself to do it at that moment.

'Incantations or poems, they're all the same. I have no time for the man who cannot face reality.'

'Maybe reality is different to each different person.'

'Rubbish.'

He took his hands out of the water and looked at them. He shook them and a shower of muddy drops scattered over the table.

'Any soap?'

I nodded and got up to fetch him some from my kit-bag. I rummaged. Behind me I could hear him rippling his fingers in the water.

'I gather from Bennett that you never went to school.'

'That's right.'

I handed him the soap and my small grey towel, then I lay down again.

'A grave error of judgement on your parents' part, I fear.'

I said nothing. He was possibly correct, but nothing on earth would have made me admit it to him. He bent low over the basin and scrubbed at his face.

'Have some clean water,' I suggested. 'I don't feel like washing.'

He paid no attention.

'It is at school we are taught to accept the burdens of manhood.'

'I was supposed to be a delicate child.'

'Leadership and service.'

He dried his face vigorously on the towel, and then began to scrub at his fingers as he had scrubbed at the knife.

'Incantations,' he said with contempt. 'Catholic?'

'No.'

'You never know with the Irish.'

He folded the towel, as no doubt he had been taught at school, and put it on the table.

'Yes,' he said thoughtfully. 'Leadership and service.'

'You lead, we serve.'

'You are very impertinent.'

'I'm sorry. I don't think I meant to be.'

'You are not, I hope, tainted with the Irish disease?'

'What's that?'

'Disaffection. Disloyalty. Epidemics flare from time to time.'

He picked up his knife and examined it with care, then, satisfied, he put it into the pouch.

'If nothing else, Moore, if nothing else, I will make a man of you.'

It sounded like a threat. He got into the flea bag and lay back and closed his eyes. The conversation, if that was what it had been, was over.

We spent three more days in the front trenches, mainly shovelling and making props. It rained a considerable amount of the time. Sometimes sleet cut into the men's bare hands, and at night there was a sharp frost that covered the bottom of the trenches with a thin film of ice. We extended the line on our left. It was hard work moving the earth, heavy with water, always crouching till one's back and shoulders ached pitifully. The men hated it and worked slowly, grumbling most of the time. For most of the day there was concentrated shelling of the German lines by our artillery. The shells screeched over our heads sometimes for hours at a time. After a while I became so used to the noise that I felt strangely unprotected when it stopped, then slowly the process of thinking had to begin again.

Bennett replaced us just after dark on the fourth day. He and his men then had to start on the unpleasant job of wiring the new line. Luckily for them our progress had been slow and there was a mere stretch of fifteen yards or so. Major Glendinning had a look at our work before we left and gave me a curt nod. I presumed he meant that it would pass muster.

I was contemplating the prospect of removing my boots when Jerry slithered round the door.

'Have a drink.'

'Yer.'

I threw the flask to him.

'Yourself?'

I shook my head.

'Gone off it?'

He unscrewed the lid and took a drink.

'I can't sleep. I thought maybe it was that.'

'Sure no one can sleep, only freaks and maniacs.'

He handed me the flask.

'Perhaps you're right.'

It was the only thing that was a positive pleasure, the feel of the alcohol creeping like a slow flame down your throat. He knelt down in front of me and began to ease off my right boot. The illness in his eyes as he smiled at me was a reflection of my own. He didn't speak. The operation took some time. It was painful and I honestly didn't know if I would ever get them back on again, my feet were so swollen.

'It's like taking a cork out of a bottle.'

He then began on the second boot. He carefully peeled off my socks. Without a word he took up the flask and poured some of the rum into the hollow of his palm and then began to massage my feet.

'Hey!'

He only grinned.

'You'll be a new man in the morning.'

'How about your own feet?'

'I don't take these things as hard as you do. Sure you were hardly let out and it raining.'

'A slight exaggeration.'

'Not far wrong.'

'I suppose not.'

He took another drink.

'I've been wanting to ask you . . .'

'What?'

'How did the old man do it?'

I couldn't think what he meant.

'You know . . . the other night.'

'Oh . . . ah . . . knife.'

'Jay.'

'Mmm.'

'Well, you have to take off your hat to him.'

'I suppose so.'

'Will I do your legs for you too?'

I shook my head. I only wanted to sleep now. My feet were floating off on some life of their own. The door opened and Sergeant Barry came in. Jerry pushed the flask into the straw and got to his feet.

'All correct, Mr. Moore. I've just checked down the lines.'

'Very good, Sergeant. Thank you.'

'Anything else, sir?'

'No.'

I found it almost impossible to keep my eyes open.

'Has this man a problem, sir?'

Jerry's eyes flickered.

'No. It's all right, Sergeant. I couldn't get my boots off. I called him in.'

'I see, sir. If I may say so, sir, it would have been more sensible to call your orderly.'

I damn well blushed.

'Thank you for your advice, Sergeant. That will be all.'

He waited at the door until Jerry had left, then he followed him out. I turned out the lamp and tried to sleep. Sleep came to my limbs but not to my mind. I saw them sitting alone,

one at each end of the long glowing table, the candlesticks, the salt cellars, the reflected flowers, the trappings of their impeccable lives between them. They would speak only when the servants were present, and then lapse into unkind silence. They all wanted me to become a man. I found it hard to grasp what exactly this entailed. God knows, one or another of them had told me often enough. I had somehow in my head the misbegotten idea that it all had something to do with the exploration of darkness. The darkness that is inside. Their voices when they spoke, polite and yet uncompromisingly vicious, would slide along the polished mahogany. Manhood perhaps when the turbulence of the human mind and the calm of the human soul can relax in each other's company. Does it matter whose son I am? After all, it is what brushes off against us after birth that makes us what we are. That was what she had seen as she watched me growing. She had watched his giving and my taking. She too had to make her contribution.

We spent four more days at the front before going back to the farm. We heard stories of massive losses along the line towards Ypres, but came across little new death ourselves. The remnants of men and animals were constantly with us. I found it hard to feel any emotion towards this debris, merely nausea. Christmas came and went, barely noticed, certainly not celebrated. Some Royal personage sent us all plum puddings, which we dutifully chewed our way through. The men had an extra ration of rum. Joy was extremely confined.

A letter arrived shortly after Christmas from my father.

My dear son,

First and foremost Christmas greetings to you. I have not come up to scratch as a correspondent, but writing letters is something that I have never enjoyed. I must, I am afraid, refer to your last, or is it only, letter to your mother. It has upset her deeply. She showed it to me, and I must admit to laughing, while admiring your literary style, but she has taken it as some contemptuous dismissal of her feelings of concern for you. I hope that you will write and make your peace with her. You must realise that she is under very great strain. All meanders on here in the usual winter fashion. The hunting has been good. Your little mare is coming along splendidly. I had got used to your company, and now find my own very unsatisfactory. I remain your loving father.

I lay on my bed and stared at the ceiling. A network of cracks patterned it, some deep black dangerous chasms, others delicate strokes like fine pencil lines on what had once been a white ceiling. If you stared long enough the lines became patterns, or faces, or a wild mélange of animals tumbling and chasing with a gaiety that didn't fit the situation in which they found themselves. Bennett hummed to himself quietly as he also read his post, and crackled the paper in his fingers impatiently.

'Oh God,' he said suddenly and dropped the pages and envelopes on to the floor beside his bed.

'What is it?'

'We are winning the war.'

'Really?'

'Really. Important people in high places are saying . . . 'Thanks to the courage and devotion to duty of our brave boys we . . .'

'. . . are winning the war. That what your people say?'

'Pride and encouragement. Reassurances. I can't help getting the feeling that what they'd really enjoy would be a tip-top hero's funeral, and a lot of medals to put in a glass case. And you know those little notices in The Times . . . in loving memory of our hero son, killed gloriously . . .'

'Oh, shut up. My father says the hunting's good.'

'What is in your head, Alexander? I never know.'

'No more do I. Nothing important, I know that. I am afraid. Not that that's very important. I really would like to remain untouched.'

'By the war?'

'That too. Everything.'

'How bizarre,' he said and then repeated it, and then went to sleep.

During that six days at the farm Major Glendinning really put the pressure on us. No one had a moment's peace from his drilling and marching. We were up at dawn and were harangued and chased from then until it was dark and time for sleeping. Severe punishments were meted out for the most trivial offences and Bennett and I were hauled over the coals if he considered we were being too lenient with the men. Our equipment and uniforms were transformed from their highly bedraggled state into one approaching orthodoxy.

The night before we were due back in the trenches Bennett and I walked back from our final briefing with the Major. A gallant moon sauntered across the sky unperturbed by the flak that rose and curved around her. It was bitterly cold and the ground crackled under our feet. The breath almost froze as it left our mouths. Bennett had been sent a pipe for Christmas and he struggled with it from time to time without much enthusiasm. At that moment the glow of it, brilliant and then fading, was the only comfortable thing around. An owl crooned. The big guns were silent and only the distant popping from what sounded like toy guns could be heard. Bennett held the pipe-stem gritted between his teeth. I could see them gleam like silver. My jaw was heavy with the cold and felt as if it were trying to drag itself away from the rest of my face. The angry bark of a fox came through the air.

'Ah,' I said, almost with pleasure.

And again it came, not too far away, confident.

'You sound so pleased.' Bennett spoke with difficulty round the stem of his pipe. A few sparks whirled from the bowl as he spoke and died of frostbite.

'I'm easy pleased, as they say at home.'

'And how much more pleased if you could jump on a horse and go and kill the damned animal!'

'Charmed.'

Another handful of flak was thrown up into the sky. The moon remained unworried.

'Beautiful.' I stretched my head back until my neck ached. 'Like very expensive fireworks.'

'Very expensive indeed.' He took the pipe out of his mouth and peered into the bowl. He didn't seem to like what he saw. He put it back in his mouth and blew through it angrily. He felt in his pocket for the matches.

'I don't think you'll ever settle down and become a pipe man.'

He grunted and struck a match. I could see his fingers were red and disfigured with chilblains. I could feel as I looked at them the intolerable itch of his chilblains in my fingers. He shook the match out and threw it on the ground.

'Damn,' he said. He took the pipe from his mouth once more and put it in his pocket.

'My father's a pipe man. The perfect pipe man. He uses it to protect him from the world. He never has to look at anyone if he doesn't want to, stares into the pipe. What's in the bowl of a pipe, for God's sake? Burning grass, that's all. You let it agitate you. That's all wrong. Anyway it makes you look like a bank manager.'

He put his hand out and took hold of my ear. He squeezed and pulled.

'Hey ... ow ...'

'A bank manager indeed, you little murderer of foxes.'

He pulled harder. I ducked away from him feeling as if I'd left half my ear in his fingers, and caught him round the left shoulder. I pushed my knee into his back. His feet nearly went from under him, but he saved himself and, turning, caught me in a bear's hug, trying to lift me from the ground. He held me so close I could feel the laughter shaking inside him.

I broke out of his grip and took hold of his wrist.

'Give me back my ear.'

'Never. Never. I'm going to smoke it in my pipe.'

'A cannibalistic bank manager, what's more.'

'Good evening, gentlemen.'

We let go of each other and each stood lonely for a moment under the amused gaze of the moon, and the accusing one of Sergeant Barry.

'Good ...'

'... evening ...'

'... evening ...'

'Good sergeant ...'

'... good ...'

Tweedledum and Tweedledee.

He glared at us and then crackled past us over the frost. We were struck with agonising laughter. We arrived at the farm trembling from the silence of the laughter and went in. It was a little less cold inside and smelt of dust and drying clothes and nameless soup. Jerry was waiting in our room. He was standing by my bed and had obviously just got up when he heard us on the stairs.

'Hail to thee blythe spirit, bird thou never wert,' said Bennett, a little intoxicated by our brush with the sergeant.

'What kept you? I've been waiting for near on an hour. Where were you?'

'The old man kept us.'

'That from heaven or near it ...'

'I'm sorry you've had to wait so long.'

'Yes.'

'... Pourest thy something ...'

'What's up with him?'

'Don't ask me.'

Bennett began to take off his clothes, dropping them around the floor as he peeled them off his body.

'Full heart,' he said. 'That's it. Full, yes.'

'Did you want something, Jerry?'

He looked at Bennett.

128

'Don't mind him, for God's sake.'

'No. Go ahead. Don't mind me. Behave as if I wasn't here.'

'If you'd shut up, perhaps that might be easier.'

I took off my greatcoat and hung it on the back of the door.

'Do you think the Major'd give me leave?'

'What now?'

'Yer.'

His hands had been clenched in his pockets. He pulled one out now and held a piece of paper towards me.

'What's this?'

I took it from him, and he shoved his hand back in his pocket again.

'If you'll excuse me, ladies and gentlemen, I will now retire.' Bennett hopped into his flea bag and shut his eyes. 'I am now asleep,' he announced. 'I hear no evil, speak no evil, see no evil. Amen.'

'Sit down, Jerry.'

He sat on the edge of my bed.

I opened the folded piece of paper. It was a letter. The words stood nervously upright on pale-blue lines. The letters were large and looped and carefully formed. Black, fading into grey sometimes, in the middle of a word when the pen needed another dipping.

Son dear I don't know what we'll do I hear from some officer the day your father is missing. How we'll do without the money coming in I do not know but it's about himself I am worried sick. Maybe they will pay on but I do not know. Missing is not dead I say it to myself all day long and night too as I cannot sleep for thinking of it. No man should die so far from home and maybe with no priest. So if it's only missing he is son dear I am hoping that you will maybe find him and if you find him maybe you could come home as I find it hard to manage with the two of ye gone. God bless you son, and let you find your father. The weather is very bad your loving Mam.

I read it twice, mainly because I didn't know what to say to Jerry, then I folded it into its folds again. I went over to him and handed it to him. His fingers were ice-cold as they touched mine.

'I don't honestly think he would.'

'Would?' He looked at me, puzzled.

'Glendinning. Leave. You wondered ...'

'Oh ... yer ... I wondered. That's right. No, I don't suppose he would.'

'I can always go and ask.' My voice didn't sound exactly hopeful. 'I will write to my father at once.'

'And what good'll that do?'

'Well, I thought if there were financial ...'

'Ah leave that, Alec ... but if you'd do the other.'

'You mean ...'

'Yes. She wants me to look for him.'

'But, Jerry, you haven't a hope in hell of finding him. He's probably ...'

'No matter. She wants me to. If he's dead itself she'll get the pension. You'll ask, won't you? If he's wounded maybe there'd be something I could do for him.'

'All right. I'll go now.'

I hated the thought of the cold and the dark and the Major, colder and darker than the night itself. I put on my coat again. Jerry didn't move. I waited by the door for a moment to see if he was going to come with me.

'I'll stay here. If he won't mind.'

'He's asleep.'

As I left the room Jerry began to sing, very low. I couldn't catch the words. His hands were still clenched in his pockets.

Major Glendinning was playing bridge with three friends, or perhaps I should call them brother officers. They sat, surprisingly, I thought, round a green baize bridge table. I wondered if someone had brought it out from England or whether it had been politely comandeered from some local château. Four well polished glasses had whiskey and soda in them and an orderly hovered discreetly in the background keeping an eye on the level in the glasses. The Major waved me to a chair until he was ready. I was not offered a drink. There was a coal fire in the grate. The heat drove my chilblains wild, which was just as lucky as otherwise I might have fallen asleep. After about ten minutes Major Glendinning was dummy. He picked up his glass and came over to me. I stood up.

'Well, Mr. Moore?' He didn't sound very pleased to see me.

'I'm sorry to bother you, sir, but one of the men has had a letter from home to say that his father is missing. I . . . ah . . . wondered, would it be possible for him to have a few days compassionate leave?'

He looked at me for a long time.

'Which man would this be?'

'Private Crowe, sir.'

He took a polite sip from his glass. His face was quite without expression.

'Ah yes. Crowe. Of course.'

'I've seen the letter, sir. It's from his mother.'

'I've no doubt.'

He stared into the fire. At the table someone was tapping his cards with a finger-nail.

'It's time, Mr. Moore, you dissociated yourself from Private Crowe.'

'I thought it was a fairly reasonable request, sir.'

'Have you considered how many men in the British Expeditionary Force have fathers, brothers, sons, cousins missing, wounded, dead? Dead? Have you?'

'Well no, sir. I was just . . .'

'The answer is no. Crowe goes to the front again tomorrow with the rest of his squalid friends.'

'I don't think . . .'

'I know you don't, Mr. Moore. That will be all.'

131

Jerry must have been listening for me. As I got halfway up the stairs I heard the door open and his steps coming towards me. He hardly stopped as we met, paused briefly and then pushed past me.

'No,' he said as he passed. It wasn't a question.

'No,' I whispered after him. That was all.

The next morning the rain was coming down in torrents and we had the worst job ever trying to get the men out for stand to. To my relief Jerry appeared, looking somewhat fragile under his pack and waterproof cape. The rain battered on their tin hats, and ran around the rims and then splashed jovially down over their shoulders and riveted to the ground with quite irrelevant gaiety. They looked a godforsaken lot. The Major obviously thought so too. He tightened his lips in displeasure as he looked at them, then he turned on his heel and went back into the farmhouse. I followed him. One of the orderlies had given him a cup of tea and he stood with his back to the fire, his hands clasped round the cup. He wasn't complaining about the milk and sugar either.

'Ah yes, Moore.' He gave me a long look filled with distaste and I knew he was thinking of the conversation we had had the night before.

I saluted.

'When will we be moving off, sir?'

He looked at his watch.

'Fifteen minutes. In this weather it'll take six or seven hours.'

'Will I fall the men out, sir?'

He looked at me surprised.

'For a cup of tea or something?'

'No,' he said, and turned round towards the fire. He dipped his head towards the mug in his hands. I knew that had Bennett asked the question the answer would have been different. The same with Sergeant Barry. I was useless as far as the men were concerned. I could neither control them nor give them comfort in any way. I saluted his back and went out leaving a ring of rain on the floor where I had been standing.

Our earlier dreary sorties to the front had given us no inkling of what it was like to be under fire. We had seen the effects all around, and each one in his own way had been either sickened or numbed. Now we were left with no safe illusions to cling to. We were all equal when faced with the cold wind of death. There was little pity left in men's hearts for the dead, only resentment that each new death was another barrier down, another step in in one's own direction.

I tried to act with composure. I obeyed and transmitted orders. A machine. Bennett on the other hand was positively gay. His macabre jokes were drowned by the sound of gunfire, the sparkle in his eyes veiled by smoke. I noticed only in the back of my mind the lack of Jerry's presence. It wasn't till we got back depleted and shaken to the farm that I allowed my mind to focus on the fact of his absence, if absence can be called a fact.

'What would be likely to have happened to Jerry?' I realised it was an odd way to phrase it, complicated, but he didn't hear anyway. He was scowling at the damp French logs which gave out very little heat and a great deal of smoke.

'Bennett.'

'I'm getting damn 'flu. I'm sure of it.'

'Tell that one to the old man and see what happens.'

'I just can't get warm. I feel as if the inside of my bones were frozen solid. And the shivers. Ever felt like that?'

'It's shock. It'll pass.'

He couldn't get ill, that I knew.

'Shock? What the hell do you mean, shock?'

'Shell shock. You know as well as I do. Heaps of people suffer from shell shock.'

'You mean I'm going off my head?'

'I didn't say . . .'

'Four or five days in bed. Hot drinks every two hours. Hot

133

water bottles changed when they cool. A couple of good books, no compulsion to read them. A fire in the bedroom, flickering on the ceiling, glowing infinitesimally all through the night so that the room never gets quite dark. Not too much to eat. Feed a cold and starve a fever. Everything just as the patient likes it and a hot whiskey and lemon last thing. The only movement, the quick stagger down the passage to adjacent W.C. 'Flu' it's called. Influenza, if you prefer.'

'I prefer to call it shock. Mind you, I'd say it would respond to the same treatment. Where's Jerry?'

'What's that?'

'Jerry. Have you seen him?'

He thought for a moment.

'No. I can't say I have. He wasn't hit though, Alec. I'm sure of that.'

'Damn.'

'Why so?'

'I think he's done a bunk.'

Bennett threw back his head and roared.

'My God, you're a nice one to be telling me that I'm suffering from shell shock. You've obviously gone right round the bend.'

'I'm serious.'

'Jerry? I mean to say . . . Oh God, the secret letter . . . What will we do?'

'What can we do except hope he gets away with it.'

We drank to that. Bennett didn't sleep all night. I could hear him turning this way and that and groaning. The next day he was bundled into the corner of an overcrowded ambulance and sent back to the base hospital. As he left the room he looked mournfully at me.

'I shall die. You'll see . . .'

'Don't be an ass, Bennett.'

'I shall die ignominiously of influenza. Not even galloping foot rot. They'll probably cure that before I go.'

I laughed, though I must say I didn't feel like it.

He raised his eyes to heaven and clasped his hands.

'God of battle, let me come back and be blown to smithereens by a shell. Don't . . . oh, don't let me die of influenza.'

They took him away.

It was Sergeant Barry who brought up the subject of Jerry's absence. I was trying to sort Bennett's gear into some order. I felt smothered by a great cloud of depression. It was very cold and sleet battered against the window and rattled down the chimney into the ashes of the dead fire. Barry came in without knocking.

'Sir.'

'Good morning, Sergeant. What can I do for you?'

I got up from the floor where I had been stowing things in Bennett's kitbag.

'It's about Private Crowe, sir. I wondered if you would have any idea as to where he might be.'

'No. Why should I?'

My voice sounded defensive.

'He would appear to have gone absent, sir.'

'Oh, surely not.'

There was a long pause. He stared at the window. The exploding hailstones made ever-changing patterns on the glass. I didn't think that would interest him.

'What . . . what makes you think . . . ?' I felt the blush starting somewhere round the back of my neck. 'Have you spoken to Major Glendinning?'

'I thought I'd come to you first, sir. I thought you might have some idea . . .'

'Well, I haven't. The men . . .'

'The men appear to know absolutely nothing, sir.'

'I see. He's a damn fool.'

'Yes, sir.'

'When did he go missing?'

'Several days back, I rather fear. When we were up at the front.'

He moved his eyes from the window to my face.

'You know what the charge will be.'

'I'm sure there's some mistake, Sergeant.'

135

'I don't see the Major looking at it like that, sir.' He smiled at me. A smile of almost sweet triumph. I wondered why he disliked me so. I knelt down again and went on packing the kitbag.

'If you've nothing to say, sir, I'll go to the Major.'

'All I have to say is there must be some mistake.'

He saluted and left the room. In a moment of complete helplessness I picked up the kitbag and threw it across the floor after him. A pointless gesture, I fully realised, that would have reassured neither Barry nor Major Glendinning.

It wasn't long before I was sent for. I took my comb from my top pocket and tidied my hair before leaving the room.

'Sorry to hear about Bennett,' said the Major when I went in. 'It may be hard to get a replacement for him just at the moment. They say they're rather pushed for junior officers at the moment. What's all this about Crowe?'

'I know no more than you do, sir. I haven't seen him since that night I spoke to you about his father.'

'He said nothing more to you?'

'No, sir.'

'He hasn't got a good record, you know.'

I remained silent.

'Has he?'

'I don't know, sir. He's as good a soldier as any of the rest.'

'That's not what I mean. He has been brought to my attention more than once. Hasn't he?'

'Well, I think there have been . . .'

'Answer me yes or no. He has been brought to my attention?'

'Yes. I suppose he has, but . . .'

'When I want suppositions I will ask for them.'

He wrote something down on the paper in front of him.

'Do you know anything about his political views?'

'No, sir.'

He looked at me, waiting.

'Sure?'

'I know nothing. How could I?'

136

'Don't take me for too much of a fool, Moore.'

He wrote something else on the paper. I couldn't make out if it was a file on Jerry or me.

'I know as well as the next man what's going on in your treacherous little country. I've heard how many Irish traitors are fighting for the Germans.'

'If they are they probably feel they're fighting for their own country.'

'Interesting, Moore, interesting. I am surprised that someone with your background should make a remark like that.'

He went to work with the pen again. Scratch, scratch across the page.

'Disaffected?'

'I don't even know the meaning of the word.'

'Ha ha ha.' He laughed reasonably amiably without looking up from what he was writing.

'So you don't think Crowe has gone to join the enemy?'

'Most certainly not, sir.'

'You say that with conviction.'

'Yes, sir.'

'So you do know a certain amount about what was going on in his head?'

'I only presume, sir, that he has gone to look for his father.'

'He was told categorically not to. Unless . . .'

He looked up at me.

'I told him what you said, sir.'

'Quite.' He put the pen down in front of him. 'I'd say the charge ultimately, if he's found, will be desertion in the face of enemy fire.'

'I'm sure he hasn't deserted, sir.'

'There our opinions differ. You know what the sentence is?'

'I swear to God he hasn't deserted, sir.'

'If he's alive we will find him. A court martial will decide the rest. That is all.'

'Yes, sir.'

'Oh, just one thing, Moore, for your own good I advise you

not to try and get in touch with him.'

'I don't know why you don't believe me.'

'You are simply not very convincing at telling either lies or the truth. Thank you.'

I wondered what Jerry had in mind. He couldn't have thought surely of turning over every khaki-clothed corpse between here and Ypres. Nor would the graves be much help. By and large it was only the officers who had their names scrawled impermanently on a cross. Miles and miles of bodies there would be when it was over. Our bodies and their bodies, not only neatly parading in graveyards, but also left in their untidiness to be turned up for years by the plough or the scavenging dog. Pigs. I could see him in my mind's eye stooping solicitously over the dead and dying. He was no taller than he had been at the age of twelve. The perfect jockey, light, resilient, unbreakable. I hated to think of him searching and knowing all the time the rules. My gun was clean. That was an accident of fate. I had killed as many men as Kitchener or French, as any officer or just plain man in the British Army. Would he, I wondered, like Glendinning, give the swift coup de grâce if it were necessary. I had admired though feared that . . . Pigs I always suspected have very nasty habits. They also eat their young. The swans would dip their black-crowned heads and watch as we raced. Sometimes she would raise herself high in the water and crack her huge wings like a whip. It was never menacing. Nothing was ever menacing within the hollow of blue hills, only perhaps the hills themselves when they would become dark and high and move nearer and nearer as if they would crush the life out of everyone who lived beneath them. I had never had any curiosity about what lay beyond the hills. Now I knew. The Somme, the Aisne, Ypres, Picardy, Flanders. Such beautiful names. He was a gentle man. He would move those unspeakable bodies with great tenderness. His father had been a small man too. I had hardly ever seen him, but I held the size of him in my mind's eye. A snipe of a man. It wouldn't take more than a few shovelfuls of Flanders clay to lose him for ever.

There we also had beautiful names. Lugnaquilla, Glencree, Kippure, Tinahely, Annamoe.

I was asleep. Drowned in the deepest of sleeps when he shook me awake. It was a struggle to escape from the grasping hands of sleep, but then I realised that they were his hands, ice-cold, that were pulling and plucking at me. He was crouching beside me. His breath brushed my cheek. It was totally dark, but I knew that no one else would be pulling at my arm like that.

'Sssh,' I said. He hadn't spoken, but the room felt as if it were full of the noise of his presence.

'I thought I'd never wake you.'

'Sssh.'

I put my hand on his sleeve. It was soaking wet, and up and up right to his shoulder, sodden.

'I'll get you some clothes,' I whispered. 'Take those off at once.' I got out of the fleabag and groped my way across the room. I found him some underclothes and a jersey belonging to Bennett. It would do for the time being. His skin was ice-cold like his hands. 'Get into my bed, it's warm.'

He sighed as he lay down.

'Anything to eat?'

'Sorry. Only brandy.'

'That'll do.'

I got the bottle from the table and went and lay down beside him. I pulled the blanket up over us both and handed him the bottle.

'How did you get here? Did anyone see you? You know they're looking for you?' I could hear him letting the brandy down as if it were water.

He took the bottle from his mouth and shoved it into my hand. 'Yes. I know they're looking for me. No one knows I'm here. You can take that as the truth.' He gave a little laugh. 'All that practice mitching from school taught me to avoid being seen by people I didn't want to see me. It was coming up the stairs here really frightened me. Jay, it did. Are you all right?'

'What do you mean am I all right?'

'I didn't like going off on you like that. I take it there was trouble?'

'Trouble isn't the word. I'm all right, but you're not. Why in hell's name did you come back?'

'There didn't seem to be any place else to go. I thought about it. Over and over. I didn't see how I could get across the Channel.'

'And you the great swimmer!'

'Maybe if I'd had a couple of bottles of that inside me I'd have swum and all.'

'Did you find him?'

'Have one yourself.'

I did. His mouth had made the bottle-mouth warm. He turned on his side and crept as close to me as possible. He was trying to steal my warmth. I put an arm round him and pulled him tight to me. He felt incredibly fragile.

'Yes,' he whispered. 'I found him. Found about. Found of.'

'Well?'

'He stepped on a land mine. I think your man Bennett might have called it galloping foot rot.' He was quiet for a long time. 'On a bloody diversionary raid.'

'I'm sorry.'

'I hardly knew him. He was always away. He liked the life. He used to polish his boots every day until it was time for him to leave again. He never did a hand's turn around the place. Polished his boots. I never seen such boots. I'll have to write and tell her.'

'They will in time. Why not leave it to them?'

'I'd like her to know I went. It'll please her that I did that.'

'The consequences . . .'

'I shit on the consequences.'

'We must get you away.'

'I'm tired.'

'If we dressed you in Bennett's uniform we might get you to the coast.'

'And then the long swim? Be your age, Alec. I'd be lucky

140

to get to the coast. Anytime I opened my mouth they'd know I wasn't an officer. I'd probably be shot on sight. Anyway, I'm tired.'

'You have to get out of here. Don't you realise . . . ?'

'Nothing. I did what she wanted me to do. I'd do it again. I've harmed no one. The British Expeditionary Force is no worse off. No one has had their dignity impaired. I'd say he's better off where he is. Lookit, Alec, at least I got up off my backside and did something.'

'You did have to choose just the wrong thing to do.'

He threw an arm across my shoulders and we lay in silence.

My warmth was spreading through him, but the hand that clasped the back of my neck was still cold as a stone fresh from the sea.

I thought he had gone to sleep. The beating of our hearts was like the cracking wings of swans lifting slowly from the lake, leaving disturbed water below.

'When we get home we'll get a place of our own.' His voice was soft with drowsiness.

'Did you ever go with a girl in the end? Like you said you wanted.'

'Time enough for that. Think of all the girls there'll be after the war and not near enough men to go round. Then we can really pick and choose. I often imagine the pleasure of drowning slowly in the huge arms of a widow of forty-five. Vast. A featherbed of a woman. None of your bony little whiners for me.'

'I will live alone.'

'What about me, hey? What about?'

'Sssh. Not even you.'

'Wouldn't you be afraid to be lonely? To be alone for ever?'

'No. I'm only afraid when I'm with other people. You and your fat widow can live near by. And there'll be the horses. We'll have them. I will give sweets to your children.'

'You'll be alone.'

'Mmm.'

'That's no way to live.'

'It's all right. My house will only be a shell for my body. I don't want anyone to breathe my air with me, to disturb my dust.'

'I wonder if it is right.'

'I don't see why not. I will behave impeccably in public. Isn't that all that matters? I'll fly whatever flag you tell me to fly from the chimney stack. Maybe I'll write soft-centred books. Sometimes my fingers itch to write, but my mind is blank. I have neither plots nor messages.'

'You'd better stick to horses so.'

'You're probably right.'

I must have dropped off to sleep for a while. He nudged me with his elbow and my eyes came stiffly open.

'I'll have another drink,' he said. 'We'll have to do something soon.'

I fumbled around for the bottle.

'You're the man of action.'

'You think. I'll act.'

'Don't be absurd, Jerry.'

'Don't argue, just think.'

He took a long drink. Too long a drink. Gently I took the bottle from his hand. Brandy trickled down his chin. He scooped at it with a finger. I put the cork back in the bottle. I caught sight of Glendinning's face in my head and I knew that we could neither outthink or outdo him. There was movement below us. A restless shuffling on the floor and then silence again. Jerry's hand gripped the back of my neck painfully.

'Think.'

He squeezed with his fingers. Sharp arrows of pain shot up behind my ears.

'Well, the way I see . . .'

'No prevaricating. No ifs and buts, Alec?'

'Yes?'

'I'm frightened.'

'No.'

'What do you mean, no? I'm frightened. I know. I can smell it off myself.'

'You've just got us mixed up. That's me you're talking about.'

'What am I to do? Hide?'

'No. It wouldn't help. Merely put off . . .'

'. . . the evil hour?'

'Quite.'

'Well?'

'There are only two alternatives.'

'Run or stay.'

'Quite.'

'You think no better than I do.'

'I've always said that.'

'Oh Jay.'

'I think you should stay. Face the . . . you know.'

'Tararaboomdeay.'

'I know it sounds disagreeable.'

'But it's what you would do.'

'I suppose so. I must be honest. I don't know. I might just try to avoid . . . evade. I think I'd be wrong.'

'Will you speak for me?'

'Of course I'll speak for you, but my voice is not very loud.'

'Shout then.'

'And Bennett. I know he will too.'

'Ah, Bennett. Bloody Bennett.'

'Why do you say that?'

'Another mighty English hero.'

'He just talks a lot. He has a warm heart.'

'With an Englishman that only means he'll cry as he shoots you.'

'I thought you liked him.'

'Ach and I do. I'll stay then if that's what you recommend. I know of no hole to hide in round here that I wouldn't be blown out of by one side or the other.'

Someone laughed suddenly downstairs, whether it was in their sleep or not it was impossible to tell.

143

'You'd better get dressed quickly and get out of here. You should go straight to Major Glendinning. Yes. Oh God, see us through this one.'

'I did the only thing.'

'I know. For you. That's all any of us ever do, I suppose.'

I disentangled myself from him and got up. Every move I made seemed to shake the house.

'There's some pretty foul water in the basin there. A wash would do you no harm. I'll find you some clothes. You can't get into those wet ones again.'

I struck a match and looked at him. He smiled at me, his eyes dazzling in the light. I lit the lamp and the room became a green cave. It was bitterly cold.

'What would I want to wash for?'

'Please yourself. Personally I always wash before an important appointment.'

Jerry leant over the side of the bed and spat on the floor.

'Brandy.'

'You've had enough.'

'I say no.'

The bottle was on the floor by the bed. He reached out for it and pulled the cork out hurriedly and threw it across the room. Rain rattled, or it could have been gunfire. He lay on the bed and drained the bottle into his mouth. His face was colourless except for black hollows under his eyes. Fear made him swallow on and on and I could only watch. Finally, with a huge gesture he threw the bottle across the room after the cork. With an explosion of sound it shattered against the wall. He, without warning, fell asleep. Voices below and movements. I still couldn't move. Steps on the stairs. The door opened and behind me O'Keefe's respectful voice.

'Is everything all right, sir?'

'Yes.'

'Mother of God.'

His feet moved across the room. He stood beside me and we both looked at Jerry stretched on the bed.

'Is he hurt, sir?'

'No.'

'Just . . . ?'

'Correct.'

He moved cautiously over to the bed.

'Poor bugger. How . . . how . . . like . . . if you wouldn't mind my asking?'

'He just came in the door. Like you did. He was very wet.' It sounded pretty inadequate somehow, true and all though it was.

'Would you have a plan, sir?'

'No, O'Keefe, I'm afraid I wouldn't. No plan.'

He scratched at the back of his neck.

'I'd say it'd be as well for yeez both if he wasn't found here.' He looked at me anxiously. He was the sort of man who knew the ins and outs of every situation.

'I don't know what to do.'

'If you would go out for a little walk. I'd like to get him out of here before the Sergeant comes. You know what I mean. He's a rough man. I maybe could hide him till he's sobered up. That way you needn't know a thing. Not a thing. Just look surprised and keep mum. Don't let the blame of his foolishness be rubbing off on you, like.'

'I have to speak for him.'

'That's one thing, sir, but aiding and abetting, that's a horse of a different colour.'

He smiled uncertainly at me.

'It'll do neither of yeez any good if he's found here. You see that?'

I nodded.

'Then,' he picked up my boots from the floor and handed them to me, 'ye'd do as well to go'.

I did as I was told. My boots were damp inside and I had a struggle to get them on. Jerry snored like a man with nothing on his mind. I picked up my greatcoat and went over to the door. I didn't like leaving the cave. My hand was on the door-handle when the door pushed open towards me and willy-nilly Sergeant Barry was with us. He could have been standing outside for some time. It was hard to tell. He had an expression of Chinese inscrutability on his face.

'Ah,' was all he said. He didn't even bother to salute me. Jerry's snore became monstrous. Barry took a step back to the threshold, never taking his eyes off Jerry, just in case he might disappear, and bellowed out into the darkness of the stairway.

'Two of you up here at the double.'

We lapsed into silence again after that and listened to the uproar below. Feet scrambled on the stairs and two soldiers, guns at the ready, almost fell into the room.

'He's under arrest.'

He nodded towards the sleeping Jerry.

'We found him here, sir. Mr. Moore was just on his way to tell the Major.'

I blushed. Barry ignored the words. The two soldiers picked him up and dragged him out of the room. He shook his head from side to side in an exhibition of protest but neither opened his eyes nor spoke.

'Bloody Fenian bastards,' said Barry to the air. 'They think they can get away with murder.'

He gathered up Jerry's wet clothes and carried them out under his arm.

I sat down. I was shaking all over and couldn't have stayed on my feet another moment.

'Well that's that,' said O'Keefe. 'Misfortunate to say the least.'

'Rather misfortunate.'

Damn shaking hands.

'I'd say there be trouble.'

'Yes.'

Shaking everywhere.

He bent down and picked up the flea bag still warm from Jerry's body and put it round my shoulders.

'I'll light the fire, sir. They'll be making tea below at any minute. I'll bring you a mug.'

He stooped and began to move things in the fireplace.

Jerry's warmth lay lightly on my shoulders. I was grateful

for it. I wished I could do as much for him. I remember no more until they came to call me to the Major. Then it was grey light everywhere and the smoke from the fire stinging my eyes. Beside me on the table was a mug, empty, except for a shining mound of tea leaves heaped against the drinking side. I combed my hair. It seemed to be the least I could do.

'So your friend has been found.'

'He came back, sir.'

He looked straight into my face and smiled.

'Let there be no prevaricating, Mr. Moore.'

An explosion of sparks flew out of the fire and glowed for a few moments on the floorboards where they fell.

'He was found in the most curious circumstances. Even a short-sighted young man like you must have noticed that.'

I thought it wise not to answer him.

'Obtuse might have been a better word to use? Hey, hey?'

'I don't know, sir.'

'You're right, Moore, you know nothing. Least of all that we are fighting a war. Do you realise what you are wearing?'

'Some sort of fancy dress, sir.'

His face went white. He picked up his cane from the table and walked over to me. He drew his arm back. I knew what was coming. The cane struck me on the right cheek, just below the eye. For a moment I felt nothing, and then, as the pain hit me, I began to sneeze. An odd reaction, I felt, and definitely lacking in dignity.

I sneezed about five times. Serious, skull-raising sneezes. He laid the cane back exactly where it had been before, then he sat down and waited for me to finish sneezing.

'I dislike physical violence as much as you do, but there are some people who will not listen to reason.'

His hands were clasped on the table in front of him. I could see that they were trembling. I could feel my face swelling, in fact see, if I looked down, the mound of reddened flesh rising with surprising speed.

'I think that you and I have different views as to what reason means.'

'I neither know nor care what your views are. You are here to fight. To submit yourself to my discipline, to army discipline, which you consistently refuse to do.'

He sighed and rubbed at a corner of one eye with a trembling finger.

'I greatly dislike the thought of a public confrontation with one of my officers. Morale suffers. Cracks open where there were none before. You are pushing me very far.'

'I truly don't intend to. I feel, though, that justice . . .'

'That is not your department. The charges against Crowe are very serious.'

'On paper.'

'Exactly. And I as his commanding officer will submit a report . . .'

'But you neither like him nor . . .'

'Nor do I like you, Mr. Moore, but, now I am speaking out of turn, so I will have to trust to your discretion, in a few days there is going to be an attack. Something none of you have experienced before. It may change the face of the war. It might win the war. It must succeed, and for it to succeed there must be no flaw in the machinery.'

'We are men.'

'Not to me. Not to the General Staff, not to the War Office.'

'Perhaps if they had regarded us as men in the first place there might have been no war.'

'A line of facile thought that is not worth the breath you use to say it.'

He got up and walked over to the window. Outside, his war was shaking the world.

'I haven't time, Moore, to engage in pointless schoolboy discussions with you. I repeat, the charges against Crowe are very serious. There is nothing you can do. As for your own position, I have no wish to discipline you severely at the moment, but I shall not hesitate in the future, no matter what the repercussions may be. Now get back to your men and do your job.'

My right eye was closing fast. My glorious war wound,

even more ignominious than Bennett's 'flu.

'I think before I go, sir, I should make things a little clearer about Private Crowe. You see he . . . I . . .'

'Get back to your men. Have I not made it abundantly clear that I want to know no more than I already do know?'

He put his right hand up and covered his eyes. A strangely appealing gesture. I never could work out whether I hated him or respected him. He touched me in the oddest ways. Perhaps one day I will be able to see the world with clarity, recognise the patterns that seem to weave and unweave themselves endlessly through life and history. Eternal recurrences.

A thaw set in and the earth, brown again for a while, sucked at our feet as we marched through the countryside. The men were low in spirit, slow to obey orders. Endless troop transports churning mud, pushed us into the ditches, breaking the formality of our ranks, covering the men with filth. They could no longer even be bothered to shout abuse. Across the grey sky from south to north came two swans. They were flying low, their wings fanning with dignity the air around. I stopped marching, embarrassed by their presence, as if some old acquaintances had dropped in to visit me at an unbearably inconvenient moment. They skimmed the bare branches of six or seven battered trees and flew obliquely across the line of soldiers. As I raised my hand in greeting the sound of a shot reached me. The front bird's neck swung for a moment from left to right and then drooped. An ugly mass of flesh and feathers fell to the ground. The men broke ranks and ran to look. The living bird faltered for a moment and then flew on, adjusting its flight upwards towards the safety of the clouds.

'Who did that?' My voice was blown back at my own face by the wind. The men were laughing in the corner of the field. They were relaxed, as they hadn't been for days.

'Who did that?'

149

They pushed at each other to see the bird. One of its wings was broken by the fall and was crumpled under the heavy body.

'A great wee shot, man. I never knew you were that handy with a gun.'

'May God protect the Kaiser if you're ever around.'

'Who the bloody hell did it?'

'I did, sir.' A small man waved his gun cheerfully at me.

'Just why?'

All the muscles in my face were trembling.

He shrugged, dismissing me and the dead swan simultaneously.

'Where's the harm?' asked someone.

I turned and walked away.

Someone made an obscene noise and then the crisp voice of the N.C.O. ordered them back into their line again. They sang all the way back to the farm.

Barry, the messenger of doom, was waiting for me. His buttons and his face shone with equal ferocity. The men scattered to their billets.

'Are you looking for me, Sergeant?'

'The Major would like a word with you, sir.'

'I'll be along right away.'

It was the same as ever before when I went into the room. Cold disapproval, a nod, the papers, the pens, the neatly folded hands.

'Everything all right, Moore?'

'Sir.'

'We move up to the front on Thursday morning. Extra supplies and ammunition must be carried. I hope that Bennett will be returning to us sometime tomorrow afternoon. He will be just in time. Sergeant Barry will take you to the stores this afternoon so that you can see what has to be taken. We will be at least ten days at the front.'

He picked up his pen and drew three straight lines on the clean piece of paper in front of him.

'Will that be all, sir?'

'Private Crowe has been sentenced to death. You will command the firing squad at eight o'clock tomorrow morning.'

At first I didn't understand what he had said. Then, suddenly, I did.

'There must be some mistake.'

'Mr. Moore, I dislike all this as much as you do. I assure you there has been no mistake.'

He tapped at the paper impatiently.

'I warned you of the seriousness of the charges. Under the present circumstances it is essential that there is no crumbling of the men's morale. Deserters must be made an example of.'

'An appeal . . .'

'There will be no appeal. Tomorrow morning at eight. Let me remind you also, Mr. Moore, that Crowe was not merely a deserter, there is a strong possibility that he might also have been a traitor.'

'Utter rubbish.'

He reddened with anger.

'Take care, young man. Wiser men than you have come to this decision. Not lightly. Men of experience. Men who know men.'

'The men won't like it.'

'I must be the judge of that.'

He drew another line.

'Our conversations follow the same pattern. You refuse to be guided.'

'You refuse to view people as anything but cattle.'

'That's what most of them are. I suppose you may learn one day.'

'I don't want to learn anything that people like you have to teach me.'

'Ah.'

His face was indifferent to me, to almost anyone.

'Eight,' he said.

'I would very much like to know what happens if I say no.'

He looked surprised.

'I am amazed you ask. If I may say so you are making a

mountain out of a molehill. You're also wasting my time. I have no desire to have you tried. It can all become most distasteful. You are pushing me very far, I warn you. How you damn Irish expect to be able to run your own country when you can't control your own wasteful emotions, I can't imagine.'

'I say no.'

'It won't save Private Crowe. You are foolishly obtuse. Think of your parents if nothing else.'

There was a very long silence while I thought of my parents.

'I shall have you shot by a firing squad and then I shall have your body shipped home to your parents. Let them give it a hero's grave.'

'Where did you learn to be so evil?'

'The world taught me. The world will teach you. You will never understand me until the day you are faced with responsible decisions to make. People's lives, people's deaths. The crumbling world waiting for your word.'

'Please God such a macabre situation will never arise.'

'Please God,' he said quite pleasantly. 'It has taken many centuries to build the society in which we live. It would be a poor thing if a handful of emotionalists were allowed to destroy it.'

'I think you exaggerate my importance. Private Crowe's.'

'Alas no. It is people like you and Crowe who cannot see the wood from the trees who cause untold damage amongst those who see nothing at all. Those who must be led.'

He stood up and picked up his cap and cane.

'I am giving you an order. Are you prepared to obey it, or face the consequences?'

'There's no hope for Jerry?'

'Jerry?'

'Private Crowe.'

'None whatsoever.'

'Then I . . .'

'Good man.'

He came over to me and touched my shoulder lightly. My body shuddered.

'In the interests of humanity, a word of advice. Tell your men to shoot straight. It's over quicker if they do. I know they do the other from the best of motives, but . .'

I nodded.

'Good chap. You know you'll see things quite differently after a while.'

I followed him out of the room.

It was late and very dark when I reached the detention camp. I had no trouble in getting into the building. The guard at the door saluted me and called over a soldier to take me to Jerry. He sat alone in a small room. A black stove in the corner rumbled, but gave out little heat. He stood up as the door was opened and then, seeing it was I, he sat down again.

'Hello.'

'Hello.'

'I'm surprised they let you come.'

'I didn't ask them.'

He smiled faintly.

'You're learning in your old age.'

'Maybe.'

'Sit down.'

There was only the bed. I sat on it and waited for words to come.

'You've heard?' he asked.

'Yes.'

'It's a shit.'

'Here.' I took the flask from my coat pocket and threw it over to him.

'You're a jewel.'

He put it standing on the table in front of him and stared at it.

'I don't think I'll have any just the same.'

'Why ever not?'

'I'll keep it for emergencies.'

I laughed.

'Suit yourself.'

'Will it be bad?'

'What damn fools we were to come, you and I.'

'We had no choice. I've never seen a man shot by a firing squad.'

'Nor I.'

'It's the waiting. Hours. Minutes. Each hour seems so long. I can't think of anything to think about, if you get me.'

'Remember.'

'I can remember nothing.'

'The lake. The swans . . .'

'Only that their wings sound like gun shots.'

'Has the priest been to see you?'

He spat on the floor.

'You mustn't do that when you meet St. Peter.'

'You've never dared remark before.'

'True.'

His fingers screwed and unscrewed nervously at the top of the flask.

'I regret what I'll never know.'

'I suppose everyone dies saying that.'

'All those race courses our horses would have won at. Newmarket, Cheltenham, Ascot.'

I reached under my coat and took my revolver in my hand.

'Longchamps.'

'Yer. You'll make a killing there. You'll have to find a jock, you know, Alec.'

'I will. Saratoga. I'll start looking when I get home. Epsom. Have a drink.'

'No. Imagine facing a firing squad with a hangover. I know if I start I'll go on. We've been friends.'

'Right.'

'That was good.'

'Very.'

'It mightn't have gone on as we expected.'

The butt was warming in my hand.

'It would.'

'I'd like to think so.'

'Play me a tune.'

He shook his head.

'They took it from me. Took everything, even my bootlaces. In case I spoiled their fun.'

'Buggers.'

'Yes.'

'Sing then.'

'Mr. Moore's night out?'

'Something like that.'

He thought for a moment and then leaned back in his chair, his eyes half-closed.

'Good men and true in this house who dwell.'

'Ah.'

'To a stranger bouchal I pray you tell
Is the priest at home . . .'

I took the damn gun out from under my coat and looked at it. It seemed in good working order. There was a slight click as I cocked it. I looked at him, but he sang on.

'The priest's at home boy and may be seen . . .'

Footsteps in the passage. I shoved the gun away. There was a murmur of voices.

'At the siege of Ross did my father fall . . .'

They passed away down the passage. No steps, no voices. I got up and moved over to where he was sitting.

'And at Gorey . . .'

The glitter of his moist unseeing eyes through the lashes. His hands lay limp on the table. I put my left hand on his. His fingers clenched around mine.

'I bear no hate against living thing,
But I love my country above my King.'

His eyes opened suddenly. They were very blue. He smiled at me.

'Now Father bless me and let me go . . .'

I shut my own eyes and pulled with my finger. As the echoing crash died I could hear running feet. He fell slowly away from me, his fingers pulling slowly out of my hand. The chair fell with him. Someone shouted. I stood quite still with my eyes shut. The echo of the shot still simmered in my ears

155

as the door opened. They took the gun away from me eventually and led me away.

They will never understand. So I say nothing. The guns throb constantly and louder up the line. The building trembles.

Because I am an officer and a gentleman they have not taken away my bootlaces or my pen, so I sit and wait and write.